PHILO FORTUNE'S AWESOME JOURNEY TO HIS COMFORT ZONE

PHILO FORTUNE'S AWESOME JOURNEY TO HIS COMFORT ZONE

JULIAN F. THOMPSON

HYPERION BOOKS FOR CHILDREN
NEW YORK

FIRST EDITION
1 3 5 7 9 10 8 6 4 2

Library of Congress Cataloging-in-Publication Data

Thompson, Julian F.
Philo Fortune's awesome journey to his comfort zone / Julian Thompson—1st ed.   p.   cm.
Summary: Seventeen-year-old Philo Fortune hits the road after high school
to see the country and to discover the source of future
financial success but instead gets kidnapped and finds love.
ISBN 0-7868-0067-4. [1. Travel—Fiction.] I. Title.
PZ7.T371596Ph   1995   [Fic]—dc20   94-24550

For Polly and for Reggie, boon companions on the
road of life, with everlasting love

The first compound sentence Philo Fortune ever read was probably the one on the lacquered sign behind his father's basement bar.

The sentence was: In God we trust; all others pay ca$h. The letters in the sentence were all black except for those in the word *God*, which were done in gold.

At first the sentence made no sense to him. Then he thought it was hilariously funny. A little later on— about the time he figured out his father put it up there tongue in cheek—it just seemed corny, man.

But he always liked the $ in *ca$h.*

"Work all June, July, and go for all of August," Philo said. "So how about it?"

Eddie Skiles was lying on his back on the floor of Philo's room, except he had his legs bent and his feet up on the seat of Philo's chair. Phi was lying on the bed.

"Go where, exactly?" Eddie said. "We gonna vote on this? The Scoper casts his ballot for the shore."

Eddie's winter habitat was shopping malls, where he scoped girls, he said.

"Scopey," Philo said, "it's not exactly that kind of trip. My parents and myself agree it also should be . . . meaningful." He swung his feet down off the bed, got up, walked over to the window, and looked out. He'd never had an awkward age; teachers used to come outside, with paper cups of coffee, to watch him playing dodgeball. But he never had become an athlete.

"I don't want to waste my time in college, if I go," he said. "I need to get a bead on America—know where to aim to make a killing. Have a plan—you know."

He was looking out the window at the neighborhood. Someone had had a plan when it was made: Name all the streets Wild Ginger Lane and Honeysuckle Terrace, and the people would forget that they were dumplings in pollution soup, floating in and out of ugly little boxes, all of which had lousy water pressure.

"I'm not sure my folks'd understand," said Eddie Skiles. "The *shore* they understand."

" 'We hold these truths to be self-evident, that all men are created equal, that they are endowed by their Creator with certain unalienable Rights, that among these are Life, Liberty, and the pursuit of Happiness.' "

Rudyard Fortune liked to read that section of the Declaration of Independence to his classes, and when he did, he'd always ask them what "the pursuit of Happiness" was meant to mean, after which he'd try to just shut up and let them talk.

"Doing pretty much your own thing?" suggested Rebecca Light, taking off her barrette and then putting it back on for the fourteenth time that day.

"Doin' *nothin'*," said Mel Foreman, checking left and right to see who laughed.

"For most people, happiness is getting stuff . . ."

"Like a new car."

"Or even something good to eat or drink."

"Or smoke . . ." (laughter). Then (muttered) ". . . laid."

"Getting *rich*," said someone suddenly, real loud.

"Yeah, that's right," said Frank Colangelo. When it came to First Amendment rights, his thing was going for the burn. "In a capitalist society, the pursuit of happiness is when a person has the right to make a living and improve himself. In other words, get rich, if possible. And nobody can stop him." He nodded hard, approvingly.

"Except you've got to have some laws," said Amy Broten, "so that—I don't know—you can't defraud the public."

"Specifically?" said Philo's dad. "Give us an example." For twenty years he'd been at war with unsupported generalities.

"Oh, like selling stuff that doesn't work, or has bad stuff in it—asbestos," Amy said. "Making people sick. *You* know."

"Like cigarettes?" And people laughed.

"A lot of people just pursuing happiness have gotten AIDS. No, really—that's not funny."

"The truth is,"—this was Frank Colangelo again—"that nowadays the country's getting foodgied up, and nothing can be done about it. All the politicians care about is how to get elected. A lot of them—and businessmen and bankers, too—are totally corrupt. People are fed up. The only ones that got the bucks and leisure time to chase a little happiness are either crooks or millionaires or both."

"All millionaires are crooks," Mel Foreman said.

3

"That's how they got to be millionaires." He rubbed his thumb against his first two fingers.

"Not always. Some of them inherited," said Amy. "Those ones didn't have to do anything at all." She had two friends who she was pretty sure were million-aires—or at least they would be when their fathers kicked.

"But they do now," said Frank. *"Now* they find these different ways to keep from paying any taxes. They cheat the rest of us poor schmoes like that and keep on getting richer."

"And happier," yelled someone from the back.

Rudyard Fortune sighed and changed the subject by asking what all the colonists had against George III anyway, that pushed them to declare their indepen-dence.

He hadn't liked what the kids said about the pursuit of happiness; he hadn't liked what they'd said for some years now. At one time, he thought that kids al-ways took the opposite point of view from their par-ents', but the present generation of dingbats sounded like his stone-age neighbors, people his own age. He wondered what was in his own son's heart of hearts. Was Phi a hopeful liberal, like his old man?

It was hard to tell. Whenever Rudyard brought up America in the '90s at home, Philo mostly rolled his eyes around. If only he'd had him in his class, he could have made him put some things in writing.

"The truth is, everybody cheats, and anybody who says he doesn't cheat's a liar," Philo said to Lisa Glat-felter, his most recent—very recent—squeeze. "I don't, though," he amended. He dropped his eyes, then smiled, and rolled them all around.

"You! You liar!" Lisa hollered, laughing. Her parents

weren't home but might be any moment. She turned toward Phi and gave him a noogie, high up on his right arm, which had been lying on the back of the sofa in her parents' den.

It hurt like hell, but Philo didn't whimper. Lisa was a Physical Girl.

"I don't cheat on *you*," he said.

"You'd better not." She knelt up on the sofa, throwing a knee across his lap to straddle it. She seized him by the ears.

This was only their third date. Anything could happen.

Lisa thought that Phi was fall-down cute. She liked to see his huge brown eyes light up—just like a little kid's. ("Oh, sure," her best friend, Stephanie, had said.) He had perfect, straight white teeth and lips like oompah-pah.

She could see that it'd soon be possible for him to have a minibeard. Think Bono, but a bigger kidder, and close up.

"So, what'll we do now?" She'd gotten off him, just like that, but was still on the couch, beside him.

He flopped onto her front.

"How about we go upstairs?" he whispered to the fourth button down on her cardigan. He imagined it to be a hidden microphone, connected to a reel-to-reel recorder in the basement, next to which crouched Jeremy, her thirteen-year-old brother.

He could hardly wait to hear how she said no.

"Before we go upstairs, you've got to bring me *flowers*, first," she said. "And take me out to *dinner*, take me for a moonlight *stroll*. We ladies like romantic men . . . ," she grinned, and straddled him again, ". . . who don't just try to grab us and go, 'giddyap.' " She bounced a half a dozen times.

"Besides," said Lisa, with another bounce or two, "my parents made me promise. That Magic Johnson business made my mother crazy."

"Mine, too," he said. "So, anytime I leave the house I have to wear a condom. Even to the store."

"You *don't*," she said, and paused. "Right now?"

"Mm-*hmm*." He nodded, smiling.

"No, you don't," she said. "Go on." But laughing, liking this.

"Do, too," he said. In fact, he'd never had a condom on but once, and he'd been home, alone.

"Prove it," Lisa said. "If you can prove it, I'll—"

"Lisa!" The front door opened, unmistakably her mother, back from another time zone, three major malls away.

"How about," he said, but softly, speaking fast, "we run out for a lobster dinner and a moonlight stroll . . . ?"

She was off his lap and sitting on the floor, with television on.

"Oh no," she said, "that doesn't count. You know I've—"

"What doesn't count?" said Jeremy, collapsing on the sofa next to Phi. "You watching *Jeopardy!*? I hate that show. What movie did you get?"

"*Dead Again*," said Philo, pocketing the tape of *Truth or Dare* they'd watched earlier. "It's a classic."

6

"Ew—what's *in* this, anyway? It tastes like *licorish,* almost."

Marietta Fortune, Philo's nine-year-old kid sister, had spread out the spaghetti on her plate like people spread out dogs to look for fleas. Working with her fork, she'd scraped a little pile of brown off to one side.

"You mean the boneless pig's-tail sections?" asked her father. "Or the little chunks of imported a hundred percent foot callus?"

"Ew, *disgusting* . . ." (squealed).

"Rud, for heaven's sake . . ." (but smiling).

"It's sausage, shrimp-for-brains," her brother said. Sometimes he felt his family had programmed conversations. That he and all the others *had* to say what they were saying. "Pure Italian sausage."

Marietta stopped her raking and looked over at him.

"You sure?" she said, suspiciously. "So, you want mine?"

"Yes and hell no," said Philo. "You know what they *put* in this stuff? A kid at school, his brother worked in this meat-packing plant? On what they call the 'gut deck'—."

"*Muh-ther* . . ."

"Changing the subject, if we may," said Sarah Fortune, putting a peanut-butter-and-banana sandwich on her daughter's place mat. It was she who'd thought of eating dinner as a family, that year. "Any luck with the Big Job Search?"

"Not exactly. Wimpy's isn't hiring. And anyway. . . ." He tried to make that last word function like a roadside sign: Good Idea Ahead.

But first he twirled spaghetti round and round his fork. *This'd* be a sign, he thought, an omen. He lifted up the fork and—*yes!* No loose ends—a *miracle!* He popped the whole load cleanly in his mouth and nodded as he chewed.

" 'And *anyway*'?" his mother repeated. She'd kept the feather cut and big, wide smile she'd worn in college where she'd made the All New England soccer team. Almost the only weight she'd gained since then took the form of black-rimmed glasses, shoved back on her head a lot. She liked to think that Philo thought of her as one of his best pals.

"Oh, yeah. Picture this," said Phi, holding up a hand, with fingers spread. "A guy with a big *plan,* of *huge* importance—I'm referring to my trip, of course—is in need of funds to finance same. He wouldn't *hear* of letting Mom and Dad step forward with the necessary cash. . . ."

"Mom, can I please be excused?" asked Marietta.

"Not yet," Sarah said. "There's good dessert." She didn't call that bribery. These were the sorts of memories a person had forever.

"How is it possible, he asks himself," Philo kept on babbling—"to work, earn money during June–July, and still reap benefits in August, while away? As a young adult, in school, he doesn't qualify (he doesn't

8

think) for such a thing as unemployment benefits, or even welfare. . . ." He thought his plan was burlap with a gold thread running through it. Simple but productive, good for the economy. He'd create new jobs. Two jobs. For him. Then let them trickle down to someone else.

Part one: wash store windows in the Marketplace, downtown. Purpose/explanation: sweat-free, stylish work, swirling Mister Squeegee back and forth to leave a shiny pane, while (better) chatting up a million passing girls.

Part two, and simultaneously: do lawns, by following this special strategy. Go to wealthy persons' houses, well before the mowing season. Ask to see the lady of the house. Offer her a free trial mowing, obligation free. Mow the rascal, do a super job; bathe self in symbolic sweat (this one time only). While showing off the job, explain that you are one of *a number of kids who've pledged to contribute half of what they earn to a new students' organization that's just starting up down at school.* Mumble its name, when asked, as if embarrassed: *Students Against Premarital Sex* (one never calls it SAPS). Then tell client *she* should set his fee, per mowing, that he'd be pleased to make *whatever she believes is fair.* Ten to one, the idiot will grossly overpay.

Part three: sell both businesses to someone needing work in August.

The short form of all that, which he offered, smiling, to his parents was: "I'm gonna go in business for myself. Mow lawns and stuff."

There was a momentary hush.

"Did I *tell* you?" Sarah broke it, gleefully, talking to her husband. "Did I *tell* you, in the hospital, and him still getting used to mother's milk and warming up the diaper? Did I *tell* you I saw a genius in this boy?"

"You did," said Rudyard. "Absolutely. And me—I

scoffed, and scoffed again. I'm so ashamed. And now, well, 'awestruck' doesn't start to say it. Wow. 'Out of the mouths . . . ,' no, hardly that. But still. *Mow lawns and stuff?"*

"Could you walk us through the process?" Sarah said to Phi, reaching out to squeeze his hand. "Tell us how you ever *thought* of that? Or was it, like they say, a blinding flash and there the whole thing was, in all its complexity?"

"What *is* this good dessert?" said Marietta. "I'll clear off, if I can get it." She rose, collected, made the journey to the sink.

"Rave on," said Philo, calmly, to his parents. He was used to this. He'd even come to like it, in a way. They'd reached an age where they could entertain themselves.

"Is this what you call *good*?" Marietta'd opened up the fridge and taken out a small cheesecake with cherries on top.

"Why couldn't you get *strawberry*? Or even plain. You *know* I hate this kind. It tastes like pukey cough stuff." She put the cake down on the table and recoiled from it.

"Now can I be excused?" She turned and started toward the living room.

But then she stopped and looked back at her family.

"Peggy told me there's a hotline you can call, anytime you hear about—or *know* about—a case of child abuse. I've got the number memorized, and you know what? I'm not afraid to use it." She grumbled off again. ". . . bet if I was in a *foster* home . . ."

"They'd feed you rusty gruel," yelled Philo after her.

"I would have liked to take a trip, in high school," Rudyard Fortune said. "I *really* would have liked to. I'd have given half my license plate collection. We talked

about it all the time." Rudyard was a victim of male pattern baldness, but only on the very summit of his flattish dome; among his other legacies were a long nose, slightly saggy cheeks, and a wet lower lip. He'd often tilt his head back when he spoke, which made him look a great deal like a llama.

"Where'd you have liked to go?" Philo asked his dad. He was eating cheesecake, still. "If you'd been able."

"California," Rudyard said. "Big Sur. Anyplace along that coast up there. Any of the beaches. Not L.A. 'California Dreamin',' Phi."

"You guys wanted to *surf*? That kind of thing?"

"No, not necessarily. I don't think it mattered. *Doing* wasn't all that much a part of it. Mostly, all we wanted was to be with other kids, just fool around."

"But didn't everyone smoke dope and stuff, back then?" Philo smiled and made his voice all deep and phony. "And participate in the *seck*-shual revolution? I mean, I'd call *that* doing, wouldn't you?"

"Oh, sure; I guess. Things got exaggerated, though, a lot. You know how people talk," his father said. "It was pretty easygoing then." He stretched his arms high over his head and made a growly sound.

"But in a *passionate* kind of way," he said. "I think we really were pursuing happiness."

"Happiness?" said Philo.

"Happiness," his father nodded. "Our vision of a new and different world. We thought that it was happening. That folks were getting it together, yep." He smiled that little smile of his, the one that made Phi look away and pick his nose, sometimes. "Oh my."

"You were my age, right? When you thought that?"

"Your age and even older. Back in college, too."

"Happiness was a warm puppy, eh, Dad?" Philo said. It was like they'd traded roles, and he'd become the grown-up in this scene. "An'—wait, I got it—one of those old VW campers with a homemade paint job."

But even as he scored with that, he also winced. Early that spring, his parents had sprung for a new— or make that an *additional*—car. One that *he* would be allowed to drive. They were going to let him take it on his trip. It was a red 1972 VW Squareback. He told his friends his mother's aunt had died and left it to her.

"So what's it to you, hotshot?"

He hadn't heard his mother come back in the dining room. Now she was standing right behind his chair. When she'd left the table, she'd picked up her book off the counter and gone into the living room, ostensibly to read. His father did the dishes when he didn't cook. Philo'd heard him say a few too many times that it was "no big deal." He never liked his friends to see his father doing dishes.

"What's *what* to me?" he asked his mom. He was pretty sure he knew exactly what she meant. She'd been listening, not reading, all this time.

"Happiness," she said. "What's happiness to *you*? What's it going to take to make my boy sing halle-lujah?"

He rolled his eyes.

"Peace on earth," he said. "And, duh, let's see. A cancer cure, an AIDS vaccine, no starving people any-where, honest politicians, perfect pollution controls, repair of the ozone layer . . . ," he started to get up, ". . . an end to global warming and to unchecked population growth, homes for—"

"No, you don't." His mother pressed both hands down on his shoulders; she leaned a lot of weight on them. He didn't have the leverage; he couldn't move. His mother (also) had a certain physicality.

12

"That's argle-bargle," Mother said. "Don't try to bull-shit your old mum."

"Okay, okay," he said, "just let me finish." He cleared his throat self-importantly.

"But seeing as none of those is very likely," he continued, "or probably even possible, I'd settle for . . . oh, half a mil, six hundred thou, a year. I'd say my comfort zone's in there, somewhere. That'll be my target, anyway. Not for right away, of course, but by 2006, when I'll be turning thirty."

"Your comfort zone?" he heard his mother say. Her hands slid off his shoulders and he heard her move back from behind his chair. Going just by sound, he thought that possibly she'd tottered.

"Uh-huh," he said. "You know—that song you used to play: 'Don't Worry—Be Happy'? Like *there.*"

"I hate to peepee on this nice parade," his father said, "but half a mil is *mucho* kale." He scratched his chest. He was wearing a Renaissance Dude T-shirt.

"How will *you* earn half a million dollars?" he went on. "I guess that anyone could make that, playing baseball in the bigs—except, because you never liked the game, or the coach, or their having practice after school, you've never really *played* much baseball. But maybe if we got some gloves and turned on the outside light and started playing catch . . ."

"I don't expect to make it playing *baseball,*" Philo said.

He'd taken his outstanding motor skills for granted all his life, but sports, as played in high school, didn't interest him. The point was not to sweat, except out by the pool.

Rudyard thought his son had sounded irritated. Was it perverse of him, he wondered, to be pleased by that?

13

"What, then?" Sarah's voice now seemed a little choked to Phi.

"We'll see," he said. He remembered those as being the most irritating words she'd said to him all through his childhood.

"You're going to be making five hundred thousand dollars a year in thirteen years, and you don't know how, yet?" she inquired.

"Not exactly," Philo said. And now he did that stretch his father'd done and made *his* growly sound.

He pushed his chair back and got up.

"This trip should clarify my thinking some," he told his parents, turning from one to the other, bowing slightly, imagining that he was Japanese.

"Clarify your thinking?" croaked his dad.

"Mm-hmmm. I imagine I'll be querying a lot of people on all sorts of different subjects. As I said to Eddie, I think this trip is going to help me get a bead on things, on *America*," he said. He liked that phrase, the hunting . . . analogy, was it?

"And Eddie, probably, will serve as your retriever," said his mom, "after you connect. He doesn't strike me as the *pointer* type."

"I guess," said Philo. "That's pretty much an open question, still. I was thinking. Maybe I'd be better off taking a different kind of person on this trip."

"One who doesn't think that Scrabble is a kind of eggs?" his father asked.

"Yeah, possibly," said Phi. "And also of the feminine persuasion, possibly."

"Forget it," said his folks, in chorus.

"If you do, you take her piggyback," said his old man.

Lying in bed that night, Phi thought about what he had said, at dinner, specifically the half a mil a year, by thirty. He'd never put his hopes in quite those words before. It didn't seem like much, considering how much a house cost in a decent part of town, and what a new car cost, and what you had to pay to send your kids to college. He'd heard his parents toss those numbers back and forth for years. And all those prices would be higher still when he was thirty.

Was it insane to think he'd ever make it, make that kind of money? Saying it was one thing, but thinking it, believing it, when you were lying there in bed and all alone, and all too terribly aware that so far in your life you hadn't broken any records, been elected anything, or heard from anyone you were some kind of genius . . .

What made him think . . . ? He turned over on the other side to find a cool spot on the bed; he'd started sweating.

He told himself the thing his mother'd used to croon when he had nightmares. That everything was okay now and would be even better in the morning. In the morning, in the morning, and, yes—fingers crossed, now—on his trip.

3

Two weeks later, Phi was sitting at his desk, hunched way over, virtually embracing what was on it, looking miserly. His big brown eyes were lighted up again, and his perfect, straight white teeth were glistening.

It was almost 10 P.M. He was using Betsy Moffitt's chem lab notes, re-creating them inside his own lab notebook. He was paying her a compliment, he'd told himself, by doing this: the sincerest form of flattery.

There were those, he realized, who'd call what he was doing at that moment cheating. Mr. Boland ("Bobo") Lonsbury, who taught him chemistry, would call it that. Or, possibly, he'd say "mithreprethenting," being delicate. And whenever Bobo's lisping voice combined with air, some fine saliva was precipitated. Phi claimed that was "a chemical reaction."

Yes, Philo knew his chemistry, all right. So he could tell himself that he was simply saving time and energy by using Betsy's notes. He didn't really like to do it, and would die if, say, his parents ever learned he did. But he'd pretty much convinced himself that outside the silly halls of academe, his actions weren't sinful but intelligent. Time, after all, was money (moola, gelt, mazuma, do-re-mi). Smart money.

There came the sound of footsteps climbing up the stairs. With practiced ease, Philo opened the top desk drawer, scraped both notebooks into it, and bellied it shut again. Fast as you could say "Chihuahua," he was studying Spanish.

Knock-knock; then, "Phi?" His father's voice. "You still awake?"

"Yeah, sure. Of course. Come in."

But he did not; he only poked his head in, leaning on the doorknob.

"Would you mind just coming down a sec?" he asked. "Hate to interrupt, but Mom and I have something that we'd like to clue you in on."

Philo nodded, made a showy check mark in the margin of his open book, and stood. "Would you mind" plus "hate to interrupt" plus "clue you in on" equaled what he always needed most to know, that he was not in any trouble—anywhere, with anyone, for any earthly reason. He sighed, in great relief.

And, to celebrate the moment, he said the duh-words of the day, "No problem."

"Just like that?" he said. "Ka-boom?"

His mother'd been laid off. She'd lost her job, been booted, fired, canned, de-salaried. There would be fallout, had to be. Mutations in the Fortune lifestyle coming up, Phi thought. Hideous deformities. Just, please God, don't let it be his tr- . . .

"Not so much ka-boom," his mother said. "More of a ka-*sob.* They really did feel bad."

She flashed her famous good-sport's grin and gave

a perky little shrug. Phi was skeptical of both. Her eyes looked worn and seamy; he could see right through her.

She'd been in charge of sales at Totswear, Inc., a company cofounded by her two good friends: Beth Hale on the creative side, and Emmy Hardy with her head for business. Now Em was taking over sales herself. Explanation: the economy, of course.

"Look," said Philo. "Marietta's fast asleep, upstairs. You don't have to put on some big act for me. What's the bottom line?"

The way he looked at it, they'd hit an iceberg. The kids were in the boats already. Now the other passengers would learn if there were any life preservers.

"In a word, *uncertainty*," his father said emphatically. "Mom's going to look for work, but it may be a while before she finds a job as . . . interesting as what she did for Hale and Hardy."

"For 'interesting,' read *lucrative*," said Sarah. "I imagine I could stick the fries and Cokes and burgers in the cardboard carryall."

"But you can go on *unemployment!*" Philo said excitedly. He hitched way forward in his chair. "And do some winky-dinky on the side. Like Nubby Behren's dad. Between his unemployment and what he picks up sealing driveways plus a little simple roofing, he's doing just about as good as he was doing building houses, having his own crew. Nub told me that himself."

"Um," his father said.

"An' I'll tell you something else: he doesn't miss the paperwork one bit, Nub said. Or sending Uncle Sugar that big chunk of everything. So, all Mom has to find is something part-time where they'd pay her cash and keep her off the books." He paused. " '*Stá bien?*"

He watched his parents shoot that look at each other. Sometimes he wondered where they thought he was—how far along the road from Peter Rabbit's briar patch, or Oz—to where it's *at*. Of course, at other times he was confused about his whereabouts himself. And theirs. Whether they'd evolved at all since everything was "groovy." He wasn't sure they could appreciate how much he tried to help them. How much he wished he could.

"I'm hoping to avoid . . . oh, that mentality," his mother said. "I'm certain I'll find something good. It just may take a little while, a lot of looking."

"A lot of poking into holes," his father said, agreeably, "to see what slithers out and coils around her ankle."

"There's something else," said Phi. This seemed to him as good a time as any. He fiddled with the volume and the tone control, hoping he could get them both exactly right, setting them at Softly and Sincerely. "About my trip."

"No, no, no," his father said. "We've passed that one around already, Mom and I. It's a go. *You* go. No earthly reason not to."

"So don't think any more about it," his mom chimed in. "You're sweet to make the offer." She made a kissy-mouth at him. "But we don't need financial help from you . . ."

"Though once you're in your 'comfort zone' . . . ," said Rudyard with a twinkle.

That phrase, regrettably from Philo's point of view, had zoomed right up the charts and now, already, was a standard. And it would be used against him for as long as Rud and Sarah knew that "Flash" came after "Jumpin' Jack."

"Well, if you change your minds," he said, to make

double certain that they never would, "I'll understand." He thought—he hoped—that was true.

"Cheese-mareez," said Lisa. "She was *fired?*"

"Negative," said Philo. "What I said was, 'lost her
job.' She was laid off. Fired's something different.
With fired, you've got yelling, slamming doors, hard
feelings afterward. This wasn't that, at all. Everybody
swore to God and hugged, from what I understand."

They were heading south on Fredericks Street,
where Lisa lived, walking home from school. His
mother had the Squareback, answering an ad.

"Daddy's had to lay three people off, but only sales-
men," Lisa said. "He's keeping everyone in Parts and
Service. He says people more and more are fixing up
the junk they usedta trade, instead of buying new Co-
rollas."

Phi considered that. He didn't ever want to be in
Parts and Service. Guys who wore their first names on
their breasts did not first-name the maître d's at better
restaurants, or hang with women who were used to
swimming sidestroke, nude, on satin sheets.

"It's scary," Philo said.

"What?" said Lisa, turning to peer up at him. There
was a hesitation in his voice she wasn't used to
hearing.

"When you think a person could—through no fault
of his own—end up in . . . Parts and Service."

"Hey, they make good money," Lisa said defensively. "You know what Daddy gets for labor, now?
Thirty-five an hour. And the guy gets half of that, or
more. They make good money, Phi. And Daddy says
they're worth every penny of it. The good ones, that
is."

He did quick calculations in his head, just for the
hell of it. Twenty bucks an hour, forty-hour week—

eight hundred bucks. Let's see, by fifty weeks a year, that's forty thousand. Sure that sounded like a lot of money to a kid, but it was *nothing*. It was what his father made for teaching school!

"Right, but—I don't know—sometimes I think about the way my parents live. Even when the two of them are working all the time, we're barely getting by. They never can relax—you know?" He looked down at her to see if she did.

"It isn't that we're suffering or anything," he said. "But if there's something that they want—let's say a cashmere sweater or a really special jacket—they can't go out and get it, just like that. I imagine *your* folks could, but—"

"Imagine this," said Lisa, flipping him the bird. "They can't. Not nowadays. My father got talked into putting money in a new development in Florida? Like, what, five years ago? A can't-miss deal, according to this meathead who's a friend of his, supposedly, down there. And for a while, it was. It's on this man-made thing they call an inland *sea*? They thought that it was gonna be a lake, and then it turned out salty? So now, guess what? Well over half the units are still empty and the stupid 'sea' is drying up on them. The interest on the loans he had to take is killing us. We used to eat out three, four times a week, but now we're calling up for pizza and he's yelling, 'What's with all the top-pings?' "

Philo shook his head and stopped dead on the side-walk.

"But he'll bounce back, your dad. He's still doing better than *his* father, isn't he? Giving his kids stuff he didn't get himself, and all. Isn't that the way it's meant to work, here in America?"

"I guess," she said. "I never thought about it much."

"And the other thing that happens is," he said. (She

thought he seemed oblivious, like in a daze.) "Out of every so-and-so-many thousand guys, probably one guy pops up and does a whole lot better than his dad. He's like a killer whale. He knows where all the food fish are; he's powerful and fast, he gulps them down and keeps on getting bigger. Lisa, I want to be that guy. I almost *have to* be."

There was an empty Diet Pepsi soda can, right in the middle of the sidewalk, lying on its side. He kicked it, hard, and it went skittering along the sidewalk, staying on it to the corner, never going out-of-bounds, up on a lawn, or on the grassy border by the curb. Yes! he thought. Oh, yes! That was borderline miraculous. He, presently a seminobody, was *going to be* the killer whale.

Eddie'd dragged him out to watch the softball game. There was this one girl, Roni, just a freshman, whom he said he had to scope.

"She's our second baseman, get a load of her," he said. "Watch how she gets down, before the pitch. She's ready for whatever's going to happen, don't you think? Isn't she a pizza-piece-a work?"

From the stands where they were sitting, Philo couldn't see whatever Eddie saw in Roni. So she could bend her knees and stick her heinie out—so what?

"She any good?" he asked, to be polite.

"I wouldn't know," said Ed. "Not yet. So far, I haven't even asked her out." He nudged Phi with his elbow.

A girl from the other team hit a soft little pop-up to the shortstop, who caught it, and Roni and the rest of them all screamed, jumped up and down, and ran right off the field and over to their bench.

"Not to change the subject, but," said Phi, "the trip

is looking good. My folks are even getting me a Mobil credit card, so we can—"

"Oh, that reminds me," Eddie said. "I meant to tell you. I can't go."

"What?" said Phi. "You're kidding me."

"I'm not," said Ed. "I'm really pissed. It isn't my idea. You'd never guess what's happening."

"What's *happening*?" said Phi. "Hey, you tell *me*." All of a sudden he felt hot and slightly nauseous. "I thought we had this planned, for God's sake. Didn't you tell me it was all arranged?"

"I thought it was," said Eddie. "Hey, look. There's Roni in the on-deck circle, see? Does that look promising, or what?"

Roni had a bat behind her neck, holding it by either end, arms bent and shoulders back. Her ample breasts were showcased well in that position. Even Philo couldn't help but notice them, not that even they could take his mind off this atomic bomb that had been dropped on him.

"Just tell me what the hell is going on, all right?" he said. "Why you can't go."

"My parents signed me up for some dumb summer program," Eddie said. "It sounds like it's the pits. First of all, it's out in Idaho, somewhere—completely in the wilderness. My father thinks I lack self-confidence, and this is meant to pump it into kids like me. Its name is On the Edge. The way it looks to me, just reading the brochure, I possibly will die out there. Either drown, fall off of a cliff, or starve. That's if a bear don't eat me first. But if I make it through, supposedly I'll be a whole lot tougher, more aggressive. Here's their motto, right? We Give 'Em What It Takes to Get It Done."

"And do your parents realize what this does to *me*,

23

my plans?" said Philo, now not only furious but hurt.

"I hate to tell you this, good buddy," Eddie said, "but I don't think they care."

"If it wasn't the last minute," Philo said. "Christ, it's almost summer! Anybody I could stand to be with for that long a time'll have their plans all made by now. I'm really up the creek, I hope they know that, Eddie. What I mean is that I hope you'll *tell* them. Work on them to change their goddamn minds."

Roni, now, was up to bat. She stuck her can out batting, too, and now that it was closer, not to mention pointed pretty much his way, Philo knew what Eddie liked about the girl. When it came to T & A, Roni looked to be a pizza-piece-a work, as Eddie'd said.

"Couldn't you take Lisa?" Eddie said. "All she ever does is hang around her pool all summer."

"My parents wouldn't stand for it," said Phi. "And when you come right down to it, I wouldn't want to take a girl. Especially that Lisa. I can't stand her; she's a pain." He certainly wasn't going to admit to Eddie that his parents had forbidden him to take her.

"You'd be, like—I don't know—responsible, I guess."

"It isn't so much that," said Phi. "It's more like, if I took a girl—assuming there was one I liked enough—well, that'd mean she's *it.* You know what I'm saying? If something better comes along, I couldn't do a thing about it; I'd be stuck. That doesn't seem American to me. To keep yourself from going after quality, the best available."

Roni hit a little grounder to the pitcher, but she ran hard down the line toward first until the pitcher threw her out. Running, she looked extra good—athletic—in control of all her assets, Philo thought.

"I hear you, my good man," said Eddie, watching her, his fine discovery, his little all-American.

It turned out that On the Edge, the program Eddie's dad was counting on to jump-start his son's testosterone production, wasn't in the state of Idaho at all.

Philo discovered that one Sunday afternoon in June, · the day before the Scoper got shipped out. The window washing and the lawns were going well by then.

"I was thinking I could maybe find out where you're bivouacked and smuggle you some ice cream or a *Penthouse,*" Philo said. "But there is no way I can drive that far. Not by myself, and with my kind of money. My mom got all these maps from AAA? Idaho is cripes' sake next to California, just about, but north."

"Then that's not where I'm going," Eddie said. "This is more like Middle West, or maybe in the South, even. Where's Indiana? Or Kentucky? We can ask my dad when we go in the house. I'll bet he knows. He had to send a check to somewhere, months ago."

Even after he found out where Eddie would really be, Philo didn't swear he'd stop and visit. He'd have to wait and see, he said. People always seem to claim they're not the sort that hold a grudge, but many of them, such as Philo, find they are.

Having to go solo on his trip changed everything. First, and maybe worst of all, was how much more expensive it'd be, with no one to go halvesies on the gas or the motel room (whenever one was called for by some social, or climatic, happening). But just about as bad was . . . well, the *sidekick* factor.

Philo was abashed to find this out, but what he felt, when Eddie wussed out on him and he drew blanks on a replacement, was somewhat less courageous. With Eddie looking on and going, "wow," Philo would say or do a lot of things he might not do alone.

But maybe he was only being normal, Everyman, he told himself. Face it—there was no *Lone* Ranger. And—he didn't mean this as an insult, but—Eddie was a natural Tonto.

"You must feel like . . . oh, some great adventurer," said Sarah Fortune. She was stretched out on her side on Philo's bed, her head upon her hand, her elbow on his pillow. She was barefoot, very tan, wearing faded jeans and her Joe Namath football jersey. The top was big and baggy, but tacklers would have slipped right off those pants of hers.

"Well, yeah, a little bit," he said, smiling, looking at and then not looking at the rolling contour of his mother's hips and playing with the thin little folder of traveler's checks that was on his desk.

"Though it's not like I'll be blasting into space or rafting through some unmapped wilderness," he added.

He'd learned a rhyme in, possibly, fifth grade: "De Soto was a Spaniard, of royal Spanish blood. He discovered the Mississippi and was buried in its mud."

26

He'd been a big fan of the Age of Exploration at the time. "Mrs. Vasco B. da Gama?" he'd inquire of his mother, bowing at the waist, pretending to sweep off a feathered hat. "I'm Sir Francis Drake."

"No," Sarah said, "but I think it's pretty brave of you to just take off, alone, without a destination. You know what it reminds me of, a little?"

"No," he said, looking at the big old suitcase sitting on the floor beside his backpack. She'd helped him pack it, and now it was ready to be closed. On the top there was a lightweight dark blue sports coat of his father's, folded. That had been his mom's idea. "There's times when you might need a jacket," she had said. "You never know." In the backpack he had stuck a box of condoms.

"You'll laugh, but . . . well, a knight, a young Round Table guy. No, no, I'm serious." But she still laughed, maybe at the face he made. "Riding out into a world where there are dragons by the score, not to mention maidens, hanging out of towers, tossing him their favors, or whatever." And she winked.

"That's me, all right," he said, and laughed himself. "Oh, absolutely. Except you made me promise to be careful. Rubber gloves for any favor catching, right? Which, of course, I did. Promise, I mean. Anyway, I've told you what this trip is all about." He feigned exasperation. "I've told you and I've told you. The only stuff I hope to catch is strictly bankable." He laughed again.

He'd decided on a question he was going to ask of adults, everywhere he went—all different kinds of adults, on the streets, in stores, wherever he could find them and go up to them, his clipboard in his hand. "If you had it to do over again—if you were starting out right now—what would you do?"

And then he had some follow-ups. "What is it that you want the most but can't afford?" was one.

27

"Who's doing best around here?" was another.

Aside from those questions, he didn't really have a plan at all.

"Well, I've noticed," Philo's mom was saying now, "that the maiden population here in town is lookin' kinda good. What's that new one's name, again? The athlete? The one you took to the fair?"

"Roni," Philo said. "Second baseperson on the soft-ball team. Yeah, she's just a freshman, but she's got a real fine personality."

"I noticed," Sarah said, again. "Outstanding. Yes, she seemed to be a lovely child." She paused. "So *out*going, and all."

And when her son looked over at her sharply, she raised her left hand off the blanket, aimed a pointer-finger gun at him, and cackled.

"Easy does it, Mom," he said.

In the morning, everybody stood outside the Fortune house to see him off.

"Don't forget to write," his father had to say while waving him good-bye.

"And remember what you swore to God you'd also do," his mother added.

His sister guessed that had to do with flossing or with manners, but in fact it was about his calling home, collect, two times a week at least.

"I'm using your TV till you get back," yelled Marietta as the Squareback left the little driveway.

For a good two minutes after pulling out of his parents' driveway, Philo didn't think of anything. It was as if his head was full of monkeys doing somersaults off swinging high trapezes—tossing, catching one another, pure excitement. He was finally doing it! He'd started on his trip!

After that first rush, he settled back and thought, Here's local hotshot Philo Fortune tooling around in his old red Squareback. *This* old red Squareback, actually; he drives it as a kind of campy little joke, sometimes—like, when his Jag is in the shop. Pretty soon, he'll take a right, go up the ramp, and tool along the interstate.

Phi was only a semiexperienced wheelman. True, he'd turned a key a lot of times, and steered a car short distances: to school, to the store, for pizza, etc. He'd also often driven to two major malls in nearby towns, sometimes with another kid for company. He'd never driven on a major highway by himself, for hours at a time.

Out on the interstate, he had three nearly empty

lanes to choose from; most everyone was coming into town, that time of day. At first he opted for the fast lane, over to the left. He felt good out there, jiggling along, the pedal to the metal.

Then he looked in his rearview mirror, where he saw the biggest truck in the history of the world, (a twenty-seven wheeler, no doubt), just inches from his wide rear window. In another moment, probably, its grille would crash into his Squareback's flat behind and mingle with his suitcase and his backpack, sleeping bag, foam pad, and freezer chest, all of which were in the cargo space behind him.

"Jeezum," he exhaled, and jerked into the middle lane before he'd even looked to see if there was any competition coming.

Providentially, there wasn't. "Oh God," he murmured, horrified at what he'd done. His palms slicked on the steering wheel; the Squareback rocked as Comstock Hardwood Furniture—at least a dozen housefuls of the stuff—went blasting by.

Philo checked the mirror, flicked the right turn signal on, and changed his lane again.

"Where's the fire?" he inquired of himself, out loud. "You got a whole month, ace. Take your time and see what's where, and how it feels, and where it's damn well *at.*"

He smiled at what he'd said, its total lack of meaning. It was good he was alone, at times. He passed what could have been a hayfield.

"Hey—amber waves of grain," he added, chuckling.

He drove along, just reeling in the miles. The scenery he saw did not inform him, one way or another. He looked at trees and fields and houses, at shopping plazas and the ugly edge of one small city. He passed a lot of signs that told him where he'd be if he got off the interstate. He stopped at two rest areas, once for gas and once to get a cup of coffee. He found both stops enjoyable. They were what someone did, while traveling, when on a major trip. You filled 'er up; you stopped for coffee—regular. He wasn't hungry when his watch said it was lunchtime, so he kept on going.

He didn't think about either money or getting a bead on America at all.

Most of the time, he thought about girls—specific girls and their bodies, and the feelings he'd had because of them. He also imagined meeting girls while he was on this trip. Girls, after all, were everywhere, all across the land (this fruited plain)—many girls who, so far, didn't even know he existed. It was neat, he thought, to know they were out there, and he was closing in on them, mile by mile by mile.

When he passed the Fairfield interchange, he realized he'd gone the whole way from the Oakland exit—twenty-seven miles—without noticing any scenery at all. What occupied his mind between those towns were his imaginings of goings-on (involving him and an imaginary girl) that might have been against the law (as well as popular) in both municipalities.

At a little after three, he pulled into a third rest area. He was hungry, then. His mom had got a bunch of cold cuts and stuck them in the freezer chest. He had turkey, and ham and cheese, and chicken bologna. He had fruit in there, and milk and OJ. In two big canvas carryalls were canned goods and some bags of chips and cookies; big jars of peanut butter and of jelly and of mayonnaise; two loaves of whole wheat bread; two rolls of toilet paper. There were also paper towels and salt and pepper; all the necessary openers; stainless steel and plastic tableware. And a note that said Bon appétit. Love, Mom.

Phi made himself two sandwiches, one turkey, one bologna. Preparing his own food, having his own food aboard his little house on wheels gave him a good feeling. He was mobile; he was also self-contained. With the backseat pushed facedown like that, he could also sleep there, in his car—and planned to. No sense wasting money on motel rooms when he didn't have to.

He ate his luncheon standing up, with his food and the container of milk laid out on the Squareback's hood, and after he'd taken the edge off his hunger, he burrowed in the glove compartment and took out the proper road map for his present whereabouts.

"There we are," he said out loud. And put a finger more or less on where he was.

"So if we get off at Taftsville . . ." He ran his finger up the interstate until it rested on the Taftsville interchange.

"And pick up Route 5, instead . . ."

Route 5 had been there years before the interstate. It headed in the same direction, pretty much.

"Yep, it's time to bag I-whachacallit. See a little local color for a change."

The interstate had gotten boring. It's just like being in a chute and shooting right along, he thought. Then he amended that. It was more like being on a *train*, he thought, an express. You were always passing through. And it was time to get away from all those monster trucks that belched out black exhaust.

The interstate, he thought, was like a blowgun, and he was just another poisoned dart.

Two heavyset women, wearing black pedal pushers and yellow sun hats, were walking by his parking space, both sucking on straws that disappeared into cardboard shake containers.

"You're smart to bring your own," said one of them

to Phi, gesturing with her big paper cup in the direction of the Squareback's hood. "Guess what this here set me back." She showed him what she had in there: a chocolate shake.

"I don't know," he said. "A dollar and a half?"

"Two twenty-*five*," the woman said. "I call that highway robbery. The soda jerk in there—they oughta have her wear a mask."

"It ain't her fault," the other woman said. "She don't reap no profits from that place. Money, it don't stick, out here. Believe me, kid; I know."

"She does, too," said her friend. "She's local. She's lived around here all her life."

"Adios," said Philo, future internationalist, to their retreating local backs.

Now that he was off the interstate and cruising down Route 5 at 50 mph or less, Philo felt that he was back in real America again.

Once upon a time, he saw, there'd been a lot of opportunities along this road. He passed garages, filling stations, restaurants, a drive-in movie theater. That they were all shut down and empty, with For Sale signs rusting on their walls or fences, only meant (to Philo) that competitors had come along and beaten them. What it didn't mean, he knew, was that Americans had ceased to eat, watch movies, fill 'em up, or have transmissions go ker-flooey.

"The people is a beast," Alexander Hamilton had said, supposedly. Phi'd read that in social studies; it had stuck. Beasts, he knew, were always hungry for all kinds of stuff.

Route 5 itself wasn't in the greatest shape. Its concrete surface had a lot of semi-mended cracks in it, tarry seams that ran this way and that and made the Squareback bump and rattle. So Philo wasn't too surprised, when he saw up ahead (and just before a sharp right curve), a flagman-figure holding one of those construction signs that can be turned around to tell approaching drivers either to Stop or Slow.

It had said Slow when he first saw it, from a distance, but by the time he got there it was Stop. Of course he did. There wasn't anyone in front of him. He formed a line of one.

While pretending to massage his forehead, Philo checked the flagman out. Clothes: jean jacket, purple baseball cap without insignia, wraparound dark glasses, baggy khaki pants, and work boots—definitely overdressed for the weather. Underneath the jacket, there was what appeared to be a sweatshirt, black, with writing on it; some of the letters were obscured, but Philo was pretty sure it said Get Out of My Light. The sweatshirt also told him something else: this flagman was a woman, almost certainly.

On account of the dark glasses, it was hard to tell exactly what she looked like. He gave her a conditional Not Bad. She had a straight, small nose and a determined-looking chin; her cheeks were smooth, unlined, unblemished, shaped decisively by cheekbones. He guessed she was about five five, perhaps a little on the chunky side, and nowhere near his mother's age. In fact, a *girl.*

Her head was not aimed straight at him, but still he had the feeling he was being stared at; he couldn't see her eyes, of course.

Moving very casually, she sauntered over to the car.

"This your vehicle?" she asked. Not like a cop, just curious. She laid her free hand on his roof.

"Not exactly," Philo said. "It's a loaner. Beggars can't be choosers, right?"

She must have liked that answer. She nodded, almost smiled.

34

"What's your destination?" Her voice was a surprise. It didn't go with unskilled labor.

"Wherever I end up," said Philo carelessly. "That way, I guess, for now." He wigwagged with his finger: up ahead.

She moved her head to look back down the road. Philo checked his mirror; another car was coming, a white Saab. The girl turned back to where she'd first been standing; she bent over and retrieved a little case—it could have been a superjumbo lunch box. Then she walked around the Squareback, opened up the passenger door, tossed her sign into the back, and parked herself beside him.

"Let's go," she said, and put her metal suitcase on the floor.

It never crossed Philo's mind to tell her to get out. Not at that point, anyway. For the moment, he was going with the flow. Hey—this was the kind of thing that happened on a trip, he told himself. The unexpected, right? He put the car in gear and off they went. His heart was pounding merrily; this was the life.

He steered around the curve, not going fast, prepared to stop, to see men working on the road. But there was no construction up ahead, no workmen anywhere. Well, now, he thought.

Next to him, the girl took off her baseball cap and shook her head. Waves of long dark hair unfolded like a cape and hit her shoulders.

"Do you mind?" she said. He thought she meant about the hair.

Not waiting for an answer, she started to undress.

Or perhaps "de-clothe" would be the way to say it. Philo's eyeballs bumped against the corners of his eyes while this was going on.

First, she removed the denim jacket, then the

sweatshirt, then a collared flannel shirt and a long-sleeved thermal undershirt, dyed lavender. That left her in a pale blue T-shirt with the letters IDMTM, in white, on the front of it, and Philo figured she was done. But no. She also took that off, which got her down to just a tight peach tank top.

Just. There wasn't any doubt about that, whatsoever. *Just.* Exactly so. Philo eighty-sixed the "chunky" out of her description; "shapely" took its place. Now he was sure she had on at least three pairs of trousers; that outer khaki pair was really, *really* baggy.

Next she opened up her metal case, took out a purple nylon duffel bag, and started folding what she'd taken off and putting it inside the duffel, piece by piece.

"That's better," she maintained when she was done. The wraparound dark glasses had stayed on, somehow, through all of that disrobing.

Philo smoothed his newly cut brown hair; he was glad he'd used a tiny dab of styling gel that morning. He smiled, to make his voice sound cool and cheery.

"Let's see," he started. "I don't have to ask you if you come here often—'cause I know you never have before. Or how you like the band—there isn't one. So how about if I cut right to the chase. Who are you, anyway? As in, what name would you be most inclined to answer to?"

He laughed and tossed his head her way, hoping that he'd see her laughing, too.

She wasn't, but she had taken off her shades, apparently to study him. Unexpectedly (given the dark hair that framed her face), her eyes were cobalt blue. The effect was quite remarkable. Philo felt like saying, "What . . . ?"

As well as beautiful (in a nonmainstream sort of way), she looked like . . . a granola; he'd never been attracted to granolas at his high school—girls who looked as if they might be *good* for you. All natural, organic, no artificial flavors. But this one made him think of . . . well, blueberry yogurt—the container, anyway. His mother'd talked him into tasting some, one time, and he'd had to say—admit—it wasn't bad at all.

"You can call me anything you want," she said. "What's in a name? How about . . . oh, *Brandi*, with an *i*? Does Brandi work for you?"

Philo wasn't any newborn; he knew when he was being ragged on. In this case there was tone as well as content. Mentally, he claimed a foul. He'd been a perfect gentleman. He'd laugh this off; that was what he'd do.

"Brandi, eh?" he said. His tone said Oh, you kidder. "And how about that IDMTM? Is that the band you're in, or something?"

"It don't matter to me," said Brandi (or whoever), slowly, as she turned her head away from him and started looking out her window.

Well, he thought. But also: Give her time, and let her settle down. His hope was she would come around as she got used to him and saw him as the *asset* that he was. The way that Lisa (almost surely) did, and Roni (with an *i*, he suddenly remembered), too.

Miles passed. They went through one small town and then another, and another. Each of them was typically American, and had a green, and a brick church, and parking meters. Most houses looked to Philo like *investments;* they were being worked on, painted, taken care of, and almost every lawn neatly trimmed.

The girl beside him didn't speak or even stir. Phi began to worry; was it possible that *ice* was forming here? Or—scary thought—might it be the girl was *mental*?

"You're awfully quiet," he said finally, much too loudly, with a sudden rush of breath. And then, a great deal softer, "For a pirate." Bait.

Aha—she turned her head in his direction, nibbled.

"A pirate?" she inquired. But, regrettably, in kind of a *You crazy?* tone of voice.

"Yeah," he said. *"You* know—you *boarded* me. Like, came on board without permission. Didn't you?"

"I guess," she said. He heard it in her voice; he'd made her smile. "Except I didn't have a cutlass in my teeth, exactly." She held up her empty hands and her bare arms, showing she had nothing up her sleeve, he guessed.

Unaccountably, he wondered if she might be ticklish.

"No," he said, "you didn't. And you didn't bonk me with your sign."

"I don't bonk," she said, and might have smiled again. "It's not my style."

He had the feeling he'd been sent a message.

"That's good to know," he said, as if he knew. "But I've still got some questions."

"Shoot," she said.

"Is there some place that you'd like to get dropped off? That's starting at the top."

"You're anxious to get rid of me," she said.

"No, not exactly," he replied, and made a nervous little laugh. "It's just that—"

"You don't have to lie," she interrupted. "If you'd rather that I wasn't in your car, just stop and I'll get out."

"I'm certainly not going to dump you out in the middle of nowhere," Philo said a little huffily. He never liked it when a person other than his sister said he was a liar.

"But you'd prefer to have your car all to yourself again," she said—persisted, really.

Philo took a breath before he spoke and decided he would try to face that question squarely. What would he actually prefer? His original plan had been to have a sidekick, company. Then Eddie'd let him down, and his parents had exercised their veto power on the Lisa/Roni long shot. In effect, they'd said he couldn't take . . . a *local* girl, wasn't that it? Nobody'd mentioned anything about a girl he met on the road. Suppose his father and his friends, en route to California years ago (supposing they had really gone), had met a girl like "Brandi" on the road. Would they have kept their car all to themselves?

"Not necessarily," said Philo casually. "It doesn't matter all that much to me. But before we settle that, another question. Where *are* you going, anyway? Maybe I could take you there."

"Maybe" he had said, and he absolutely meant it. One thing he was not about to do was traffic in the c word. Not cocaine, *commitment*. He was much, much, *much* too smart to ever make commitments. Or, if he did, to feel he had to stick to them. Not that any girl had asked him to so far.

"The truth is," said the girl, "that I'm not going anywhere particular. I'm just going—and observing. Seeking, hoping in a way, but not expecting. So, how about I flip it back to *you*? What's *your* destination? Like, specifically?"

He'd dodged that question once before, and he decided to keep dodging. She couldn't make him tell her anything. He wasn't going to say, "Oh, nowhere in particular" as she had done—tell the truth, in other words. Nor was he going to spill his guts about the purpose of his trip. Not to a girl he'd met only a little while before. An . . . okay, *physically attractive* girl, but one who could be a granola. Who might not know a CD—certificate of deposit—from a CPA.

"Oh, a bunch of different places," he said smoothly. "I plan to stop in Garston, for example. Maybe stay a day or two." He'd seen a town by that name on the map—it looked to be a little city, almost, from the dot—and, more recently, on a sign that stated it was sixty-something miles ahead of them.

"But I don't intend to make it there tonight. I plan to sleep in someone's field or forest—that, or right here in the car. I've got a sleeping bag." He thumbed into the space behind them.

He imagined she'd tell him sayonara then.

"That sounds as if you're saying I can do that, too. Do what you do for a while," she said. "Or am I missing something?"

For a second there, he panicked—felt a little trapped, which was ridiculous. He could still say no.

Before he answered, he looked over at her one more time. Hmmm.

"Sure, you can ride along," he said. "We'll see how it works out. Just so you realize what you're getting into." Not that *he* did, but (he hoped) that sounded cool.

"No one has that kind of knowledge," said the girl. "It'd take away the point of everything. But if you mean I shouldn't count on being comfortable, or having a good time, or even enjoying your company—believe me, I'm not."

Well, he thought, so she's a kidder, after all. That was okay—better than okay, quite fine. He liked some offbeat humor now and then, as much as anyone. In

40

fact, he hated when a girl got serious. Not that one ever had.

He was nodding, thinking, well, hey, this possibly could work out very well.

"I guess I ought to tell you now," she said. "Sorry, but—my name's not really Brandi. You can call me Thee or Thea, but it's really Theodora." She paused. " 'Beloved of the gods,' it means." Another pause. "Isn't that a howl?"

Philo'd never known a girl called Thee or Thea. Those were names he'd never said before. Same with Theodora, though it kind of rang a bell.

"You're kidding me," he said.

"Uh-uh," she said. "I *was*—before, when I said Brandi. That was just a silly little joke. But no, not now, not anymore. You're doing me a kindness, so I have to tell the truth." She paused and scratched her knee. "Now, what's *your* name?" He could tell she was smiling. "I'd like to know who I'm indebted to."

"Philo Fortune—Phi," said Phi. "And it's no big deal. I'm just giving you a lift. To Garston." But then it hit him that he might be doing more than that. "Uh—I've got some stuff to eat, back there. You can have some, too, I guess."

Maybe she'd insist he stop, so she could buy food for herself. He'd bet anything that Tonto didn't sponge off the Lone Ranger.

"I've got my own," she said. "Most people in this country eat too much, and most of that is garbage."

"Well, so they say," said Phi. "But still—American

fast food must fill some pretty basic human need, it seems to me. You see what happened when McDonald's opened up in—Moscow, was it? You see the pictures of those lines?"

"Next time you stop for gas, I'll pay," she said. "That's only fair. Me and my stuff must weigh about one twenty-five. If I had to ship us UPS, that'd cost a bundle."

Philo guessed she mustn't have been listening that well. But hell, he'd take her money.

"I'd like to figure out what's next," he said. "The next fast-food sensation. Mexican was nothing; then it gets enormous in no time at all. My father said some guy invented hot dogs in the 1930s. Can you imagine what *he* must have made? Just on that one item?"

He thought a moment. Then he said, "I wonder. Can you *patent* food? Does someone own the rights to pizza?"

Thea didn't answer; she was back to looking out the window. Probably, he thought, she didn't know or care. Girls had their interests, but when it came to interest *rates* . . . he shook his head and sighed.

Rolling up Route 5, however, Philo found he was enjoying having Thea in the car. She wasn't Eddie, but she *was* an audience.

"You know a word I like?" he said. *"Entrepreneur."* He said it slowly: *on-truh-prun-ur.* "Doesn't that sound cool? You know what one is, exactly? I looked it up in my dad's big dictionary. Last year, I think it was. Go on, take a guess."

"Let's see," she said. "I'm assuming that it's French, correct?" He nodded yes; he guessed it was. "So, I'll say 'pimp.' "

He made a face. "Not quite. It's 'a person who organizes and manages any enterprise, especially a business, usually with considerable initiative and risk,' " he quoted.

"Like I said," said Theodora.

About twenty miles before they got to Garston, Philo decided it was time to do back roads, back-country roads, the thinnest of the thin blue lines that snaked across his road map. They were looking for a place to spend the night.

Philo was a trifle yippy on this section of the program. He'd never done much camping out, except in his and friends' backyards, about the time he was Sir Francis Drake. The only wild things in those neighborhoods were squirrels and sparrows and Gay Hurlbut's brother Leon, bassist in a heavy metal band.

But way out in the country there'd be deer and bear and other bumpers, stuff that had escaped from zoos and circuses, possibly including snakes. Say hello to rabid foxes and raccoons and porcupines, good buddies. Howdy, Farmer Brown's big mean old bull.

"You know what might be good to find?" he said. "A haystack." Haystacks, he believed, were the habitat of farmers' daughters and French girls.

"Right," she said. She must have thought he was kidding. "Maybe if we went to Amish country . . . I slept inside a barn on bales, once. That was pretty nice, except for itchy."

"Yeah," he said, as in Of course it would be. Then he cleared his throat. "Do you camp out a lot?"

"Everywhere I go," she said. "Just about. Though 'camp' may be a little sweet for what I do, sometimes. Last night I used a Dumpster full of cardboard."

"No," said Phi. "Come on. A Dumpster?"

"Sure," she said. "Right outside this health food store. It was just for flattened cardboard boxes, really neat. Clean and kinda springy."

44

"God." He shook his head. "A Dumpster."

"Look!" She sat up straight, looking out of her window, looking *back,* now. *"There . . ."*

He braked, while looking over, seeing nothing different.

"You passed a good place, maybe. Stop—no kidding. Now back up."

He couldn't guess what she had seen. Another Dumpster? But he did as he'd been told.

"It's just a little ways. On the other side of the bridge. Right here."

He didn't get it. What was "right here" was a place where the otherwise narrow shoulder of the road had widened out. Two cars could park there, side by side, and all wheels off the road. Right here?

"Pull in," she told him. "This must be a place where people come to fish. It could be perfect. Let's go look."

They left the car and followed a worn pathway to the brook, or what Philo would have called a little river. It ran right through what he'd have called the woods.

"Neat," she said. "A fireplace and all." She nodded at a ring of blackened rocks set near the water. "This is nice. You got a tent?"

"Uh, no," said Phi. "I figured I'd just use the vehicle." That safely off the ground, glass-and-metal-sided little house. That lockable interior.

"Okay," she said. "I'll take the room with running water, then." She gestured, showing that she meant somewhere down here, down by the brook. She squatted right beside it, scooped a little water in her palm, and tasted it.

"Mmm," she said. "It's good."

Philo, standing, rubbed his hands together, trying to think what he should say or do. He was pretty sure his mom had not packed any charcoal lighter stuff or newspapers, so he wasn't going to volunteer to build a fire.

"You hungry?" he came up with.

"Not really," she replied. "I think I'll do a little wash, before it gets too dark." She started back up toward the car. "I'll get my stuff."

Phi followed her and watched her pull her case and duffel from the car. Laundry? She was going to do the *laundry*? Here?

"I won't pollute our drinking water," Thea said, and smiled. "I'll go downstream a ways."

"Downstream," said Philo. "Sure."

He shifted weight. "Maybe I'll . . . explore a little. Over that way. Upstream." He made a motion with one hand in that direction, proving that he knew which end was up.

"You do that," Thea said. "Have fun." And she was gone, skipping down the path as if she'd lived there all her life, he thought. He wasn't conscious of the fact, but he was frowning.

Philo didn't take right off. He guessed he ought to go upstream, just in case she asked him what was up there. (". . . couldn't believe my eyes: a huge casino and an arcade! Oh, sure.")

Too bad he couldn't pan for gold instead, he thought. Except he'd read it was a stupid waste of time these days—that even guys who knew what they were doing made about the same as some kid working at a Burger King. Nobody found, like, nuggets anymore; all they got—the lucky ones—were flakes, like little *dandruff* gold.

Shaking his head, he crossed the road and started grudging through the woods, upstream.

It turned out not to be unpleasant, after all. With the brook right there, he didn't have to worry that he might get lost. And once he was doing it, actually moving his body and stretching his legs and sucking down a few lungfuls of uncontaminated air, he felt surprisingly relaxed and happy—*good.* Because he was so well coordinated, he didn't slip or stumble, and he noticed it was . . . pretty, in the woods.

He walked down to the edge of the brook and peered at it, at the running water, stuck a finger into it, and licked the finger. Okay: nice cool water. The bottom of the brook was stones and gravel near the shore, but there were places toward the middle where you couldn't see the bottom. He imagined that was where the fish hung out.

He wondered if a fish enjoyed itself. Was a deer happy? In cartoons, they almost always were. But in real life most animals just slept and ate and hid from people and had sex, though just at certain times, he'd learned in bio. Most of the time, they didn't want to. It was hard imagining not wanting to—have sex, that is. Like, all the time. How come they called *them* animals?

Probably a lion always enjoyed being king of the beasts, though (he thought). "The people is a beast" jumped back into his mind again. So were "the people" happy? Or was it just their kings, the lions—and the killer whales? Good question—and he thought he knew the answer. It was (he thought) the scary one.

He decided he'd gone far enough. He could be trespassing on someone's land—someone with a gun. And anyway, he ought to get back to the car; he remembered that he hadn't locked it. It could have been completely stripped while he'd been gone. How often would a cop drive down a thin blue line like this one?

Back at the Squareback, however, everything was

fine; the car and all his stuff were there, intact, inviolate. Probably nobody'd even driven by. So what could he do now?

He could always eat—but then he thought it might be good to wait and have his meal when Thea had hers. That would seem to her to be a friendly, thoughtful gesture on his part. And eating with another person was a way of bonding with that person. That was the reason for the business lunch, he guessed—and why guys took girls out to dinner. You could turn on a girl with food, as Lisa'd said.

At the present time, the shape and depth of his relationship with Thea was still . . . in the works and unestablished. It'd be smart for him to give her ample opportunity to show him who she really was and how she'd be, for him—what kind of a companion. Once he knew that, he'd decide if he would let her go along with him, past Garston. Assuming that she wanted to, of course. He was not at all sure that would be the case.

He leaned against the car a while, and then got in it, drummed his fingers on the steering wheel, caressed the horn, and reached for and pulled out a road map. But he already knew where he was going, so he put the map back in the glove compartment and got out of the car again.

Waiting for a girl, he told himself, was about the most boring thing in the whole world. So why not move himself downstream and watch her do her laundry? There'd been a program on TV—or was it a commercial?—where this guy and girl got friendly in a Laundromat and later on got married. He locked the car and headed down the bank. It *had* been a commercial.

The thought of sneaking up on her and giving her a scare occurred to him almost at once. Girls acted like it made them mad, to have the wits scared out of them, but Philo was convinced they loved that kind of thing. Girls actually *expected* guys to scare them, tickle them, even gross them out. He'd cracked old Eddie up, one time, by going, "Stop it, stop it, stop it!" in a real high, girlie-sounding whine, and then replying, "Shut up, or I *will*," in a deep bass, macho growl.

He started walking quietly, bent over, watching where he stepped; pussyfooting, it occurred to him to say. He angled to the right, a little farther from the stream; there was a knob of ground that he could stay behind, so that she couldn't see him.

He heard her humming on the other side of it. Ideally, she would have her back to him, and he'd be able to get pretty close to her before he screamed his scream, or whatever he decided to do. Even grab her, maybe. But, he thought, suppose she happens to be looking up this way? The surprise would be completely ruined.

But, hey (he thought), there was another way. What he could do, while still completely out of sight, was make a lot of weird, inhuman noise, sounding like a herd of water buffalo or something. She'd become alarmed and maybe even start to run, and as she did (or even if she didn't), he could then come charging from the underbrush. She'd have a cow, at first, and then be so relieved . . . no telling what she'd do!

He nodded, liking that. He heard her humming still, and making splashing, washing sounds. No time like the present. He saw a piece of deadwood, as big as an oversized baseball bat, so he picked it up and started grunting and snarfling ("Ee-YUNK! Ee-YUNK! Ee-YUNK!"), beating that old limb against a hollow tree trunk, and kicking at the loose rocks on the ground.

And then he started moaning horribly and bellowing ("HOO-gah! HOO-gah! HOO-gah!"), after which he just exploded from his hiding place, leaping over that small knob, and charging toward the brook, full tilt, still bent way over, fingers up on both sides of his head, like horns.

His expectation was that if she wasn't on her feet and running, she'd be kneeling on the bank still, frozen there, with perhaps some dripping garment in her hands.

Instead of that, however, she was standing *in* the brook, leaning slightly forward at the waist and facing him, the water lapping against the top part of her thighs. The one thing he had right was that in addition to a fist-size stone there *was* some sort of garment in her hands that she'd apparently been rinsing in the water.

It was the only garment touching any part of her, however; the beloved of the gods was statuesque, for the most part smooth as marble, and completely naked.

A final "HOO-gah" perished in his throat, dead of strangulation. Philo stopped and stared; his mind groped desperately for something slick to say. He was too dinged out to even look away.

She, meanwhile, had dropped the rock and now walked slowly toward the bank, more or less in his direction, wringing out what proved to be a pair of multicolored briefs. She moved unhurriedly, making no attempt to cover up.

"Philo Fortune," she said calmly, "back from *up*-stream, I presume. What's the matter with you, anyway? Was I meant to think you'd lost your mind, or what?"

She spread the briefs out on a branch with other briefs and tops and socks on it. Then she bent, got dry things from her case and duffel, and started getting dressed.

"You look as if you'd never seen a person doing

wash before." Her little smile was not so much seductive or amused, as pitying, he thought.

"Gah—*wash*," he said inanely, as his vocal chords came back on-line. "Hey, look, I'm sorry. I had no idea
. . ." He hated knowing he was blushing.

No idea. He'd had no idea that she'd be naked; no, indeed, he hadn't. If he had, he would have acted very differently. He would have still been up there, but on his belly, hidden by the brush atop that little knob, quiet as a mouse. He would have stayed there till she left, most likely, taken his good time, really had a *look* at her.

"Oh, you had *some* idea, all right," she said. "Just not a very novel or engaging one. What was *I* meant to do? Go 'eek'? Fall over in a faint? I don't know why, but I expected—make that hoped for—more from you. Than something quite so puerile."

Phi could not believe his ears. His head was spinning. *Puerile?*

"Hey, lighten up," he muttered, rushing up reserves indignantly, defensively. "It was just a little fun, is all. No call to dial—what is it?—nine-one-one?"

She looked at him some more. He thought that Lisa's dad would eyeball someone's trade-in—say, an old Tercel—that way.

"You're right," she said, at last. "Why shouldn't you do . . . well, exactly as you did?" She smiled. "After all, you *are* my benefactor—*and* a member of my generation."

He wasn't sure if she was mocking him or not. He didn't think so; her smile, this time, had seemed sincere. Maybe if he cooled it, now, made nice, his goof would be forgotten.

"Let me help you with your stuff," he said. "Maybe we could build a fire. Get it dried before it's even time for bed."

"All right," she said. "That'd be a help. If you could grab my case and duffel, I'll pick up the wash. But it'll dry out hanging overnight; we don't need a fire. Not unless you plan to cook."

"Cook?" said Philo. "Me?" She didn't realize what a joke *that* was. "Oh no. In summer, I eat strictly cold."

As would anyone, he thought, except Mark Trail. Especially a geek like him, who didn't even own a pack of matches, come to think of it.

Thea's metal case contained two little plastic bags of food. She ate from both of them, using just her fingers. To drink, she went and dipped cool water from the stream in one cupped palm. When she was finished nibbling, the bags were not a whole lot emptier. He thought their contents looked granola-ish.

He had two sandwiches again, and milk, and Champs potato chips, the only kind his mother bought. He offered her the bag and much to his surprise she took it, studied the ingredients, and grabbed a little handful, nodding thanks. So then he tried her with Fig Newtons, which he also loved; she wrinkled up her nose at them. "Too sugary," she said.

As he was finishing his meal, he trotted out an Old Reliable. The one in which you rave about not hair and eyes or clothes, but personality—and character.

"There's something that I've got to tell you," he began. "And it's this: You are *unique. Amazing.* I've known a lot of girls, but no one who comes close to being anything like you. I think you're really special."

"Oh?" she said. "How so?"

She didn't melt or throw herself at him, but she also didn't put a finger down her throat.

"It's a *style* thing," he explained, basting every word with thick sincerity. "This amazing cool you've got.

Where absolutely nothing's going to bother you or throw you off your game. It's your *integrity*, I guess." He looked away and shook his head, as if he simply couldn't find words good enough to say how wonderful she was.

"I don't mean this in a bad way—understand?" he finally said. "But it's like you're way up there, somewhere. Like on another plane." He raised a hand above his head and wagged it back and forth, palm down, denoting altitude—above *him*, even. The strange thing was, he almost . . . no, forget it.

"Most people," he went on, "you're pretty sure there's some way you can get to them. Not you. Other people, they've got buttons you can push. Or, like with that car of mine, there's special places that you've got to use, if you want to jack 'em up."

"You're always on the lookout for such places," Thea said. He thought he saw her lip ends twitch—just a faint suggestion of a smile.

"Damn right," he said. "That's basic. Example: with my teachers, back in school. I study them as much as the material. What turns them on, what turns them off. Know them *and* what they emphasize in class, and you've got a win-win situation."

"You must do very well in school," she said.

He realized that the focus of this conversation had been switched, from her to him. But that was not all bad. He'd hit her with a major compliment, now she was showing interest in . . . well, *him*. How he thought and operated; how he *did*. This was not surprising. Of course she'd want to know.

"I do," he said. "Gradewise, I'm right there; I get it done. I look at grades as a credential. If anybody wants to know 'Can he produce?' a bunch of A's will tell him 'You're damn right he can.' While we're in school, we kids compete for grades. But in hardly any time at all, it won't be grades, but salaries, promotions—all the things that go with makin' it, big time."

"Uh-huh," she said, while nodding. (And nodding, where he came from, meant approval.) "So that sounds as if such things as wealth and power are two major goals of yours. Are they *it,* or have you got some others?"

"Hey, of course I do," he said. He wanted her to know that killer-whales-to-be could also be a lot of fun . . . and even cuddly.

"I've got a lot of other goals. Enjoying life, for one—playing with the toys I'll have. And having special people near to me, loyal friends and, most of all, the best, most beautiful, exciting woman in the world."

He grinned and raised both hands, palms up, as if to say, "That's all."

She was looking at him steadily, taking all this in, he thought, maybe even memorizing him. And as he sat there, the object of her lovely, level, blue-eyed gaze, it popped into his mind that maybe she, this Theodora, was the woman he'd just described. She was cool and gorgeous and excited him *a lot.* And even if he couldn't recollect them fully, he'd already seen her assets—all of them.

Might this not be fate (he asked himself)? An example of that great good luck that all successful operators have?

Would this accidental meeting prove to be a bigger benefit than any others he would reap, this trip?

"Well," she said, getting to her feet. "This is quite amazing. Let me ask you something, Philo Fortune. Have you ever wondered if there might be someone, somewhere on this earth, who's just like you? Who thinks and does and feels the same things you do? A spiritual twin, you could call it, who might be—I don't

54

know—an Eskimo or Ethiopian, who doesn't even speak your language but, in many ways, is *you*?"

"Yes," he said, although he never had. "I have. I wonder that, like, all the time!"

Now she was back to dressing, adding clothes, taking things from her duffel bag and putting them on: a second pair of pants, her Get Out of My Light sweatshirt, and the denim jacket.

"I thought I'd sleep down there," she said, gesturing in that direction. "Under those spruces, where it's nice and soft." Then she nodded toward the Squareback. "You're going to stretch out in the back, you said?"

"Yeah, fine," he said. "But—getting back to what you said about how it's *amazing*? And then you asked me if I'd thought about my 'spiritual twin' and I said yes? So, *what's* amazing? What'd you mean by that?"

"Oh, I'm not sure I ought to say," she said.

"Come on," he said. "No fair. You've *got* to say. I promise I'll behave." This, he thought, was too incredible for words.

"All right." She sighed. "What's amazing is that you and I are total opposites. All the things you want and value are the very things I scorn—can't stand. I think that's quite remarkable, almost unbelievable, don't you? That we're like *anti*-twins, or something. Like each other, inside out." She shook her head and smiled at him.

"Good night," she said, quite cheerfully. "Sleep well. I'll see you in the morning."

Philo stood there by the car. *His* goddamn car, he told himself. The light was failing fast, and his face had darkened with the day. He scowled.

"I'll see you in the morning," she had said.

The hell you will, he thought. And he jerked open the driver's door and grumped into the car, reaching in his pocket for the keys.

Was she a piece of work, or what? Compared to him, who was (as she had said herself) her benefactor? So she can't stand the things he wants and values, eh? Well, how about (for instance) transportation? He hadn't ever seen *her* walking, when she had a chance to drive—be driven, actually.

He put the key in the ignition, but he didn't turn it. He'd wait for her to fall asleep. The Squareback's engine didn't make much noise, and the babble of the brook would help cover it. In the morning, she'd come bouncing up that little path, and—oops! Imagine that—no car!

Her "anti-twin" would be long gone; he wouldn't be a sitting duck for her to dump on, anymore. This'd be good. Her "total opposite" would get to Garston fresh as any daisy, while she'd probably have to trudge at least ten miles before she even had a chance to hitch a ride. Would *her* fine, scornful ass be draggin'? Hey, you bet it would!

He sat there, very much involved with being pissed. At first, he kept on picking at his outrage, twisting the knife embedded in his pride, making the hurt flare up each time it threatened to die down.

Want to know the truth? he asked himself. He was thrilled to be *her* total opposite.

But, before total darkness came, a little voice from way back in his head, a voice that sounded an awful lot like his mother's, whispered, "Opposites attract."

He shifted in his seat and sat up straighter. And then, instead of Mom's, he heard Thea's voice: "Good night. Sleep well. *I want to* see you in the morning."

Well. So he'd appended three small words—so what? The meaning had been there, before, embedded in her tone of voice (now that he recalled it). She wanted him to have a good night's sleep. She wanted him to share another day with her. She was attracted by . . . well, *him,* her opposite. She wanted him.

That put a rather different spin on everything. While it might be true that they were not in sync on certain matters, it was also true that disagreements added spice to a relationship. Arguments—and making up, especially—were sexy. And there was something further to remember: people change, evolve; they learn from one another. Particularly girls, from guys.

Another thought piled on. A little while before, when he'd been really steaming still, he'd imagined Thea walking all the way to Garston. And when he'd had that thought about her fine ass draggin', he'd visualized it, too. Her ass! Its smooth and round and utterly

outrageous cheekiness! And something else: one totally outstanding breast, in profile, too, as she came
wading from the brook and turned to spread that pair
of underpants out on the branch.

What sort of man would turn his Squareback's back
on her unique topography? he asked himself. And the
answer was: some very different sort than Philo (lover-
of-beloveds) Fortune.

Indeed, now that he thought some more about it,
he faced the fact that he was simply not the kind of
person who left girls alone in woods, off very second-
ary roads. There was too much danger, way out here,
from predatory beasts and falling limbs or trees and
rockslides. In other words, from *everything*—from animals and vegetables and minerals.

After more time passed, and it was truly night, he left
the driver's seat and crawled into the back. After lock-
ing all the doors and cracking one front window
slightly, he unrolled his pad and wriggled into his
sleeping bag.

Before he fell asleep, he thought again of Theodora,
down there underneath those spruces. She didn't
have a pad or sleeping bag, and he didn't think that
she was armed, though possibly she might be. But it
had been her choice to go down there; at least she
wasn't in a Dumpster.

He was glad he hadn't driven off, when he'd been
tempted to. It was *him* to be magnanimous, he
thought.

He came wide awake at half past five and found, to
his surprise, that it was daylight, just about. A day with
much potential lay ahead of him. What would happen
when they got to Garston? Between here and Garston?
After Garston?

Lots of things could go, like, either way. He'd always thought his trip would be exciting, but here it was, only the second day, and the gauge read "unbelievable." already. Had Eddie missed the *QEII* or what?

His stomach growled. It always had demanded food first thing in the morning. So he ate, as usual. And then, again as usual, he took a walk and did the next thing on his morning schedule—though much more awkwardly, self-consciously, than usual.

When he returned (from quite a ways upstream), he took the little path down to the spruce grove. There was Thea, sure enough, all curled up and fast asleep, her purple baseball cap on backward, her head upon her purple duffel. He decided not to wake her, but he left his roll of toilet paper on the ground, a little ways from where she lay.

It wasn't a bouquet of flowers or a lobster dinner, but . . . this one wasn't Lisa, either. And he was oddly glad of that.

Philo's watch said quarter after seven when Thea trudged up from the grove, her duffel bag in one hand and the TP in the other. He was sitting on the ground, his legs crossed and his back against the Squareback's bumper. His mom did yoga meditation, and he'd learned this was the way you sat to do it. He'd tried the routine for a while, to please her, but it hadn't really worked for him; his mind was much too active, really, to stay empty, as she'd said it should. For his mantra, he had chosen "IBM."

Why was he making like a lotus, then, knowing Thea'd be on her way? Oh, on account of one thing that he knew: you never know.

She smiled and waved the roll at him. She looked as if she'd put in fourteen hours on a feather bed.

"Did you have your breakfast yet?" she asked, looking down at him. She didn't nibble on the lotus, but still, she'd come to him; she'd been attracted.

"Yep. You?" he said, unwinding, standing up.

"Uh-huh." She nodded cheerfully.

He walked, a little stiffly, to the driver's side, now imagining he had on cowboy boots and dusty chaps, a neckerchief.

"Let's saddle up, then," he suggested. "Time's a-wastin', missy."

Philo's plan had been that he would hold his tongue and give her time to say whatever she was going to say. He'd give her all the time she needed. He wasn't going to prompt her.

It took a good ten miles.

"Me at off pissed are really you," she finally said.

Philo popped his brows and said, "Say, what?" although it just about made sense.

"The way you'd say it is, 'You really are pissed off at me,' " she said. "But because I'm your anti-twin, I had to say it backward. I meant to say it as a question, though. You are, aren't you?"

It *would* be him to smile, he thought, and so he did.

"Mmm—yes and no," he said. With him, the truth *did* out especially when it appeared to have potential usefulness.

"I shouldn't have used the word 'scorn,' " she said. "That was a little strident of me, don't you think? 'Scorn' sort of agitates."

"Well, yes, I'd say it does," he said. "It's got some hatefulness in there, I'd say. Kind of a disgust-o-rama."

"I hope you didn't take it personally," she said. "You don't disgust me as a *person.*"

"Oh, whoopee," Philo said, but softly, meaning: give me more, why don't you?

60

"Money and possessions, *they* disgust me," she went on. "But, clearly, you don't have that much." She swirled a hand around, taking in the Squareback and its contents. "Fancy living, phoniness—I hate both of them. Keeping up with the Joneses."

Philo glanced into the rearview mirror. Then he thought: that was the only place he'd ever want to see the Joneses, somewhere way behind him.

"If I don't disgust you personally," he said, "what *do* you think of me?"

When she didn't answer right away, he added, in a sappy voice, "I let you use my bathroom tissue, didn't I?"

Out of the corner of his eye, he saw her smile and nod.

"Yes, and that was nice of you," she said. He could tell that she was serious. "Deeds count more than words, you know. I guess it's possible you're really virtuous, even if you say there's all this stuff you want to have."

"Virtuous?" he said. He knew the word, knew what it meant, all right. It was just . . . he'd never heard it used before, in conversation. He thought it was a *Scarlet Letter*–era kind of word.

(He didn't recollect, of course, that he had sounded just the same when, talking with his parents, he'd said, "Happiness?")

"Yeah," she said. "Like, full of virtue. Which is the only good, in my opinion. Virtue, that is."

"The *only* good?" said Phi. "Come on."

"Well, name another one," she said.

"Another one?" he echoed. "How about . . . ." He tried to think of something cool that also went with "good." "How about, say, *sex*?"

"Sex?" she said. She didn't laugh. She seemed to think it over, gnawing on a knuckle. "I'd say sex is sort

61

of a good. A very minor one. Or, put it this way: it's not a *good,* because virtue is the only good. But it's something people can enjoy." She paused. "Or let's say *should* enjoy. It's a perfectly decent animal pleasure."

They seemed to have gotten away from talking about him, and what she really thought of him, but that worked for Phi, because of what they'd gotten onto. His past experience with girls seemed to suggest that the more a girl was willing to talk about sex, the more sex she might be willing to have, try out, perhaps as fuel for future conversations.

"Oh, look," said Thea, now. "I guess we're coming into Garston."

And so it did appear. All of a sudden there were traffic lights ahead, and both sides of Route 5 were lined with an array of auto dealerships, fast-food franchises, family restaurants, outlet stores, and motels of various ages, sizes, and complexities.

"I guess the center's still a ways ahead," she said. But she'd undone her seat belt and now was kneeling up and turned around, grabbing at the cargo in the space behind them. One by one, she pulled her bag and case and sign into the front.

"I'd like it if you let me off *down*town," she said. "You know—wherever there's stores and sidewalks and all that. And people walking around. But if you weren't planning to go downtown, you can just let me off anywhere."

Philo suddenly recalled that he had said that he was only giving her a lift—to Garston. She obviously had taken that as *it,* as all he was going to do. That, when they got to Garston, that would be The End. Apparently, to her, this conversation they'd been having, about scorn and disgust, and him and virtue, and then (finally) sex had been nothing but a way to pass the time. To her, the stuff they'd said wasn't on the way to anywhere. If she really was attracted to him, she was doing great at making sure it didn't show.

What he clearly had to do was get another subject going, other than good-bye. And he didn't have much time.

"So, what are you planning to do here, anyway?" he said. "If you don't mind my asking."

"Do?" she said. "Not much. Doing's not the point, with me. I just try to live a certain way, is all."

"But you've got to do *something*," Philo insisted. "Or don't you?" Perhaps, he thought, her folks are really rich. In his experience, at school, it was mostly rich kids who put down possessions, *stuff.*

"Sure I do," she said. They'd been stopped by a red light. "I support myself. I only had a little baby-sitting money, when I started out." She sounded more polite than interested.

"Where was that?" said Phi. "The place you started from. You're still in high school, aren't you? When d'you have to be back home? And, how long have you been . . . doing what you're doing?"

He had to laugh. This wasn't him. "God, I'm babbling," he said.

The light had changed to green. She'd looked away from him while he was asking all those questions— turned and started looking out of her side window.

Another red light and they stopped again.

"I do peoples' likenesses," she said, her head still turned away. "In charcoal. They give me money for my sketches. That's what I'll be doing here." Now she also sounded bored.

"Ah," said Philo. "You're an *artist.* Interesting. But not surprising, not at all. And how much do you get

63

for an original Theodora?" He thought he sounded like a guy his father's age, an adult trying to show an interest in some kid.

She made some sound or other. There was a giant truck beside them.

"How much?" he said. "I couldn't hear."

"Five dollars," she said loudly, clearly. "I don't like to talk about it. That's not why I'm doing what I'm doing. I'm not trying to make a lot of money."

By that time, they were there. This *was* the downtown area: sidewalks, stores, a movie house. He couldn't just ignore it, keep on driving. He saw an empty parking space and slid the Squareback into it. Across the street: the U.S. post office.

"This is it, I guess," he said. "The heart of downtown Garston. So, where are you going to spend the night?"

It was like a nightmare. Every line that passed his lips was dumber than the one before, less cool, almost the opposite of him, or how he hoped to be, in any case.

She finally turned and looked at him.

"Who knows?" she said. "A park?" She craned her neck, perhaps to look for one. "Or maybe I'll find another nice Dumpster. What do you care, anyway? I might even take a room, if I make lots of money. Or possibly I'll meet somebody who can put me up."

Philo found he hated that idea.

"You going to use your sign again?" he grumped— and ducked his head in its direction.

"Who knows?" she said again. "Sometimes it works quite well." She dropped her eyes and smiled that little smile of hers.

"You ought to be careful," Philo said. "No kidding. Not everyone you stop is going to be a perfect gentleman." He had to smile, himself. "Like me."

"Well, maybe I'll go back to where we spent last night," she said. "I could get a ride, I'll bet, partway."

"Don't be ridiculous," he said.

"That's not ridiculous. I thought that it was nice out there. I thoroughly enjoyed myself."

He took a deep, deep breath.

"Well, maybe we could . . . oh, agree to *meet* somewhere." He checked his watch. "It isn't even nine o'clock, yet. At *I* don't know—say, six or so? And I could drive us back out there."

There. He'd done it. He'd as much as said he wanted them to stick together—wanted her to stay with him. He'd been the one who brought it up—the beggar almost, you could say. Now watch him get shot down in flames.

But she'd *said* she'd thoroughly enjoyed herself. And "thoroughly" meant in all particulars, to him. And at all times, as well.

"You?" she said. Her eyebrows were way up. "You'd want to stay out there again? Scrunched up in your car?"

"Sure," he said. "I know *I* can't afford a motel room."

"I don't know," she said. She picked her case up off the floor and fiddled with its handle.

"Nothing against you," she said to Philo now, once again looking squarely at him, her blue eyes aimed straight into his brown ones. "But I wasn't planning to spend time with anyone. Except, perhaps, a dog. That's if I found a nice one. In a pound, or something—or a stray."

Now Philo did the eyebrow thing, and smiled.

"Don't laugh," she said. "I'm serious. Everyone can learn a lot from dogs—in terms of living naturally. They have very simple tastes; they're very active physically. And if they're not mistreated, they're extremely virtuous. Dogs aren't greedy, unlike most kids I know."

"Look," said Philo. "I like dogs, myself. A lot. But that's beside the point, right now. Which is—the *point* is—do you want to meet me here at six tonight? Or, if not at six, at any other time? Just tell me yes or no."

She dropped her eyes, to think about it. Philo couldn't wait to hear how she'd say no. Her baby blues came up to him again.

"Yes," she said. Not warmly, maybe, but decisively.

He wished he could have stayed and watched her do her thing, without her knowing he was there—with him invisible. He was curious about this little moneymaking scheme of hers: how she'd attract her customers, how long it took to do a sketch, whether cops would ever give her a hard time.

As soon as he heard what she charged, he did some quick-as-lightning calculations. At ten minutes a sketch and averaging three an hour, if she worked ten-hour days, including weekends, she'd be capable of thousand-dollar weeks. Of course that was assuming there was that much raw material: two hundred different faces, willing to be gotten down in black and white.

That'd be great money, Philo thought, considering it's no-sweat, sit-down work, with maybe twenty minutes off per hour. Better, all in all, than Parts and Service, buddy.

Philo whistled as he drove away. He was looking for a place where he could pick the brains of Greater Garston. He was confident that here, and then in other towns and cities, he could find the basic information that he needed: where to fish for wealth and power in the 1990s—and what to use for bait.

One-point-seven miles from where he said so long to Thea, Philo spied a shopping plaza.

By using lots of wood and brick and lanterns (not to mention gables), the designer of this little money-magnet had managed to give the place a definite Colonial village aura. It didn't hurt that very much in plain sight down the road was the Witch Hill Country Club.

Although the plaza had a major supermarket as its anchor store, the other spaces—it seemed to Phi— were leased to businesspeople who had targeted an upscale clientele. He smiled and nodded at the sight of Randall: Ironmonger; LeMasters Sporting Goods; The Perfect Lie ("Grog and Grille"); Boutique Brigitte (ladies' fashions); Hardware by Harrison; and The Literary Lion (books and magazines). It almost seemed the Squareback was sucked in and parked itself.

Philo grabbed his book bag from behind the seat and took his clipboard out of it.

Brace yourself, America: here comes a Fortune (hunter).

"Good morning, sir," said Philo to the sitting duck outside the supermarket. "I'm conducting a survey for Operation Bootstraps, which is a statewide high school career enhancement organization. And I was wondering if you'd mind answering a few quick questions."

He had his blue Bic pen uncapped and poised above the sheet of three-hole, wide-lined filler paper on his clipboard. At the top of the page he'd already scribbled, barely legibly, Garston #1.

The man he was addressing was slouched behind

the wheel of an enormous light blue Cadillac. He had on a flat white linen golf cap (the type Ben Hogan used to wear), dark clip-on glasses, and an Izod shirt along with slacks that matched the color of the car exactly. Philo guessed—correctly—he was waiting for his wife.

"For *what*?" he said unpleasantly. His face was deeply lined, but smoothly shaved, except he seemed to have a lot of nose hair. The lit cigar he lifted to his mouth was big enough to be a lamp base; his liver-spotted hand was burdened by a diamond pinky ring.

Even taking off a point or two for looks, this guy scored high in Philo's rating system; lots of things about him shouted Big Success!

"For Operation Bootstraps," Phi repeated, "a state-wide high school career enhancement organization. Basically, we're kids who have a deep apprecia—"

"Career *enhancement*, eh?" the man said, interrupting, with a sneer. "Let me tell you something has to do with that, with *your* career enhancement, sonny. *Clothes make the man.* You understand what I'm saying? I should know, you know. Apparel was my life for thirty-seven years. You kids, you want to get ahead? For Christ's sake, put on something decent, something with a little class built into it. Look the part of what you wanta be."

"Excuse me?" Philo said.

"Take now, for instance," said the man. "You come waltzing up to me and say you've got some questions, right? But look at how you're dressed, in dungarees, just like some kinda bum." He pointed with his lit cigar at Philo, top to bottom. "Career enhancement, is it?" he inquired. "Hey, don't make me laugh. I'd *maybe* hire you to sweep up, nights, the way *you* look, young man."

"But I'm not asking for a *job*," said Philo, with a little clarifying laugh. So he had blue jeans on, a red-and-blue striped Rugby shirt (white collar), and Spalding hightops (carefully unlaced).

"I've just got," he said, "some questions that I'd like—"

"You don't get the point I'm making," said the man, breaking in again. "You wanta ask me questions, you wanta work for me, you wanta take my daughter out— what you gotta do, before, is *dress* like me, you understand? Rule number one, before you even put your foot insida door is: Dress like the guy you want a favor from. Or you can just forget it." He moved his head, and although Philo couldn't see his eyes, he felt he'd been dismissed, that he'd lost the man's attention.

"Anyway, here comes my wife," he threw past Phi's left ear.

Philo turned part way around and saw a woman pushing a loaded shopping cart and bearing down on him. She was wearing a white tennis dress, no socks, and light blue sneakers, along with quite a lot of wrist and finger jewelry. She also wore one of those long-billed fisherman's caps, a tan one with a shiny black visor. Her legs were lumpier than Phi was used to looking at.

"Harold!" she cried out as she approached. "Gimme the *key,* all right? I got a nice young *turkey.* What's this kid want, anyway? You finished your *cigar,* yet?"

"Never mind the kid," her husband said. "I'm done with him; he wanted some advice." He stuck the cigar (which was now no longer than a small salami) back into his mouth, which freed his hands to take the key from the ignition and hand it out to her. "Here." He wrapped that in a puff of smoke. "Whoever heard of eating turkey in the month of August? You remember what I told you, now!" The last seven words were aimed at Phi's retreating back.

He, however, didn't bother to acknowledge them. The guy had proved to be a jerk; Philo had better things to think about, like Thea.

Thea. He wondered if she might be sketching someone at that very moment. Possibly. But probably the hours from twelve to two would be her busiest, when people went to lunch. They could get each other into it: "Come on. Let's get her to do both of us. I will if *you* will." Like that. He bet she was real good. He found he kind of missed her, having her around.

He hoped she had a real good day, made a ton of money.

Garston #1 had been too old; that had been his problem. He couldn't deal with blue jeans; to him, a pair of Levi's were like turkey in the month of August.

But, just to be on the safe side, he wrote "Dress like the guy you want a favor from" in his atrocious handwriting and slid that sheet of paper under all the others on his clipboard.

When Philo got him in his sights, Garston #2 was getting ready to try to hoist an outdoor gas grill—the big deluxe one with the spice rack/cutting board/umbrella holder on it—into the back of a Ford Aerostar van.

"Hi," said Phi, prancing up, giving him the friendly puppy treatment. "Let me lend a hand with that." He put his clipboard on the ground.

"Oh, thanks," the fellow said. He had on bib overalls, which made him look a little country. But peeking out from under their cuffs were a brown pair of Clarks Explorers, a shoe that Philo had admired in his parents' L. L. Bean catalog, and therefore knew cost more than fifty bucks *apiece.*

"I told Rod Harrison that I could handle it all right,"

the well-shod man explained with a self-deprecatory little laugh, "but I'm afraid I may have overreached myself."

They bent, together, got their grips on it. "Sideways, don't you think?" the man suggested. "Ready? Here we go. That's fine. I thank you very, very much."

He stuck out a hand, and Philo shook it firmly, while looking the man squarely in the eye. Then he switched his stare to focus on the clipboard on the ground.

"I don't suppose you'd have a moment . . . ," he began.

The fellow laughed again. "How could I not?" he said. Behind big horn-rimmed glasses he had clear, untroubled dark blue eyes and he was losing hair in front. Philo pegged him at a youthful forty-five and guessed he owned a summer home nearby.

"I just hope you aren't going to ask about *(a)* politics, or *(b)* religion," said the man and laughed a third time. He found a red bandanna in an inner pocket that he used to wipe his hands. "But what else is there, when you come right down to it? Now that only fools believe in unsafe sex."

"Never fear," said Philo, and he rattled off the Operation Bootstraps intro.

"Now, here's my question," he continued. "If you were starting out, right now—had just graduated college, or whatever—what, exactly, would you *do*?"

"What would I do as a career?" the fellow said. "If I were starting out right now, but had my present knowledge of myself and, yes, the *world*? Oh, Lord. That's something of a toughie." He looked off into space and seemed to think it over.

"Well, I believe I might grow Christmas trees," he said. "That seems like such a simple, cozy thing to do. You don't have to mingle with the public, and you can stay at home—instead of running all around the world, as I do now. In point of fact, I have looked into Christmas trees—called the state extension service fellow. I have the land for it; we have a summer place on fifty acres, twelve miles thataway." He pointed toward the hills beyond the golf course. "And when I wasn't planting trees, or shaping them, or seeing to their harvesting, I suppose I'd want to write. I was an English major, years ago, at Yale. I've always had a kind of hankering to take a shot at writing."

"Writing?" Philo said. "You mean, like writing books? Our English teacher made us try to write a screenplay; he said that's where the money is, in writing for the movies. It was fun, but really pretty hard, I thought. And awfully risky as a job—wouldn't it be? I mean, suppose you wrote a screenplay, or a book, and then you couldn't sell it?"

The man in the bib overalls had cocked his head to one side, listening to Philo. He looked like a healthy, well-trained hunting dog. But it turned out he wasn't interested in tracking down . . . a major movie contract, for example.

"I'd do poetry," he said, and smiled. He pronounced it "poytree." "Nobody's ever made a nickel, doing that. Except for Frost, I guess, and maybe Auden. It's something that you do because you love to do it. I *like* my present work—although it has its ups and downs—but I believe I'd *love* to be a poet."

"If you don't mind my asking," Philo said, "what do you do now?"

"I buy and sell antiques," the fellow said. "Together with my wife. We meet a lot of interesting people, and there *is* a bit of profit in it."

"But it isn't something you'd recommend to someone starting out," said Phi. "A boy or girl who hoped to make a lot of money."

"Oh, dear, no." The man was getting set to step into

his van and drive away. "As far as I can see, there's only one sure way to get a lot of money. Of course it isn't easy; at times, it's even damned hard labor. But it's worked for centuries, it worked for me, and it'll still be working on the day that Armageddon dawns . . ."

He settled in the driver's seat and snapped his seat belt on. Phi had his pen point pressing hard against the three-hole lined.

". . . and that's to *marry* it," the fellow said, smiling merrily and waving as he drove away.

"An' another job I'd go for would be airline pilot," said the round man in the porkpie hat and short-sleeved shirt, a folded copy of the *National Enquirer* held tightly underneath one arm. He was sitting on the bench outside the bookstore, and he'd waved Phi over, gotten him to sit.

"Now lemme tell you why," he said portentously. "Two reasons." He held up a pair of stubby fingers, none too clean. "Correction. Make that three." And he snapped up another.

Philo's mind was wandering. He imagined Theodora trying to sketch a face like this guy's. The man was such a porker—jowly, with those little slits of eyes. If she was smart, she'd always make her subjects better-looking than they really were and, when it was possible, a little bit like someone famous. He knew this tuna'd love it if she made him look like what's-his-name, the guy from Desert Storm, the general, that Schwarzkopf.

"For one, they got these rules that say they shouldn't work too hard. Can you believe it?" said the fat guy. "What they're meant to be is safety regs, but what they really are is goldbrick rules made up by former airline pilots in the FAA, who wanta do some favors for their buddies."

74

Philo wished and wished he'd just ignored this man, that he hadn't let himself get trapped there on that bench.

". . . they also"—Fatty dropped his voice and looked around to make completely sure that no one else would hear what he was just about to say—"got amazing benefits, like making out with all them little cuties which they're calling flight attendants, nowadays. I'll tell ya, kid, I don't know why it works this way, but when you put a woman in an air-a-plane, in uniform, she right away gets so damn hot to trot she . . ."

Philo wrote down "pilot" and then "asshole" under Garston #8, keeping the clipboard angled so the fat guy couldn't read what he had written. At the next break in the action, he was going to eat some lunch.

". . . by no means least, there's what they make a year," the man was saying. "Fifty-seven five to start! How does that sound, kid?" And, whipping out his *National Enquirer* he slapped Phi smartly on the thigh.

"Great," said Philo, leaping up. "And, you've been a big help, sir. On behalf of high school students all around the state, I thank you very much."

The man now touched his hat brim with his paper, making a salute to Phi, and maybe to all other high school students, in and out of state. "Glad to do my part," he said. "Education always was a thing I had an interest in. In fact, I useta think I might go into teaching. I know I coulda done a better job than some of them you've got in there today. I'll tell you one thing: I'd demand respect—and get it, too. If you're a people-person—"

"Sure," said Philo, smiling, on the move. "I'm sure you would have."

He headed for his car to get that lunch.

Six hours later, he was thinking that the local water must contain some chemicals that zonk those portions of the brain where good ideas were born and raised. This was the kind of garbage he'd heard, all afternoon, in answer to his three main questions:

- "If I had it to do over? Hey, you know I'd do exactly what I'm doing now: sell kitchen cabinets, appliances, and countertops."

- ". . . sure as hell stay single, tell you that much!"

- ". . . to catch on with the postal service, probably. You're not a millionaire but you got security and benefits right up the bippy . . ."

- "Who's doing best? The lawyers and the politicians and whoever's dealing drugs, I guess . . ."

- ". . . the crooks, the doctors, and the millionaires . . ."

- ". . . someone like me who gets along real good with all the guys at work, and has a *super* family at home . . ."

- ". . . you'll be surprised: the guy that owns the Mobil service station on the highway . . ."

- ". . . maybe two more babies . . ."

- ". . . a week in Vegas with two six-foot show-girls . . ."

- ". . . one of them new wall-to-wall TVs . . ."

He'd scribbled all this nonsense down, thinking maybe he could use it in a social studies paper, senior year. Title: "The Decline and Fall of American Ambition, or A. Hamilton Was Right!" He wanted to get out of Garston—get Thea and get out of Garston. Basically, get Thea. He hopped into his car and headed back downtown.

Philo parked the Squareback, looked both ways, and slowly, safely, crossed the street.

He didn't see her right away. In fact, the sidewalk—the place he'd let her off—was empty. He looked up the block and down. There were some people strolling, ogling shopwindows, and some others striding purposefully along. But there was no one doing sketches, no one being sketched. No Theodora.

Well. He checked his watch. It said 5:58—so he was early. A bell began to toll; it was tolling in the tower of a large brick church they'd passed when they drove into town. So. For that one denomination, anyway, it now *was* six o'clock.

Phi looked back across the street; maybe she'd

changed sides on him, knowing which direction he'd be coming from. Maybe she was standing over there right now, laughing at how he hadn't noticed her before, when he parked. But no, she wasn't. There wasn't any girl, or any sign, or any purple duffel bag, or any metal case. There wasn't any Thea, whatsoever.

Knowing that she'd recognize the Squareback and, presumably, hang out by it till he got back, Phi went off looking for the girl. Being female, she might get some jollies out of being hunted, he decided. For no good reason, he went right, instead of left.

When he'd gone five blocks, he stopped and turned around; he'd gotten out of Garston center, into outskirts. The businesses were furniture emporia and tire warehouses, the sort of places that you'd drive to get to.

She wasn't by the car when he got back to it, so he went some blocks the other way. No luck in that direction, either.

When it got to be six-thirty, he admitted it was possible he'd been stood up. He conceded that, conceivably, she wasn't going to meet him, that she'd never planned on meeting him, that as soon as he was out of sight this morning, she had hitched a ride with someone else—having quickly flushed his image from her mind. But then he told himself she wasn't, well, that kind of girl. The kind who'd look at you and lie.

Having thought all that, he decided he would lean against the car and give her fifteen minutes more.

During that . . . moratorium, a wild (but possible) solution/explanation came to him. She could have had a really rotten (or absurdly busy) day, and had decided to knock off at (for example) four o'clock. And then decided to hitch back to where they spent the night before! (Going back there *was* a thing they'd talked about; she'd actually brought it up that morning.) She'd figure even if she couldn't get a ride the whole way there, he'd come along, eventually, and pick her up.

So, at a quarter of seven, he started to retrace his steps. There was still a lot of daylight left. He knew he wouldn't miss her on the road. He wouldn't even pass another car, along the way, in case she might be in it.

But she wasn't out there hitching on the highway, nor did he find her hiking on the narrow country road. When he pulled onto the shoulder by the bridge, he felt a sinking certainty she wasn't there. He beeped the horn, resisting hopelessness, but when he stepped out of the car, he knew at once he was the only person anywhere around. He felt the most alone he'd ever been in his entire life.

He had a funny feeling in his chest, another in his stomach, but still he made himself go down the path, pass by the spruces that had sheltered her the night before, and keep on going downstream, to the pond where she had gone to do her wash. He stood there looking at the empty surface of the water as it slid on by.

A weird idea occurred to him. He'd had a sort of crazy day—a really crazy *rotten* day in most respects, since he'd let Thea off. The answers to his questions hadn't been that great, and he had spent a lot of his time in that mall thinking about a girl who probably hadn't been thinking about him at all. It seemed that for some reason or other, he didn't have much luck with certain kinds of girls.

The weird idea was: maybe he could change his luck. Maybe if he made himself do something pretty hard, like strip and walk into this cold and slightly scary water (just as Thea had), that it (the act) would make him different and more special (more akin to special, different girls, like Thea). So that later on, on this trip or up the road of life, if he met *other* Theas, they would see him differently—and better.

Before he had a chance to change his mind, he got off all his clothes and waded in. (If he was acting like some veggie New Age simp, so what? No one would ever know.) The water was real cold, all right, and the bottom wasn't comfortable to walk on. But he kept on going to the darkest, deepest part—almost to his waist it was, out there—and sat down suddenly, dropping below the surface and then bouncing up again, flinging water from his face and hair.

His body tingled and he felt extremely clean. And happy. Pure and simple. He waded back to shore, then turned around, went back, and dunked himself again. It was as if his life—a huge, confusing, and complex equation—had been simplified to one small mindless dot of naked, joyful *good*. Corny as it was to say, he felt completely different, new.

He came out a second time, slipped on his hightops and his jeans. As he did, he kept on looking back at where he'd been, hating that he had to go and leave the moment and the feeling, pick up daily life again. So what next? he wondered.

He knew that he was going to stay the night. Not that she was going to come, or anything. He couldn't, like, *expect* that, or anything. He got into the car to eat; it was close to eight o'clock. Not much later it was dark, so he moved into the back and got inside his sleeping bag. There really wasn't anything to do.

But when he settled down to sleep, he didn't lock the doors.

When Phi was wakened by the morning light, he groaned.
He almost always groaned, the first thing in the morning; he'd decided, at some point in time, it was the grown-up thing to do. But on this day, there were some solid reasons he was not a happy camper.

One: the Squareback's floor, even with a pad on it, was hard as A.P. physics. As well as far from king-size.

Two: what he was hearing was the pitter-patter-pat of steady rain upon the Skewbee's not-tin roof.

Three: he was beginning to have certain second thoughts, while also feeling very sorry for himself.

He lay there, staring at the Squareback's ceiling as that tide of second thoughts rolled in. It seemed to him that possibly this trip had been a Big Mistake, the quintessential Dumb Idea. What was he really going to learn about America, or Opportunity, or (even) Happiness, gypsying around from nowhere-town to nothing-city, asking people (who were, more than likely, idiots) a bunch of idiotic questions?

And—when you got realistic—what were the chances that he'd meet a normal, friendly girl along the way, a girl who'd make the trip some *fun*? Who'd help him move his piece to—shall we say?—Orgasmic Gardens, on the big board game of life? Chances were, the only girls who wouldn't be locked in to other stuff (a job, or extra school, or getting gorgeous tans by someone's private pool) would be . . . well, weirdos, like that Thea had turned out to be. Girls who tell you that they're into virtue, and then turn around and lie right through their teeth.

Maybe what he ought to do, he thought, was point the round nose of the Squareback toward that concentration camp where Eddie was imprisoned. Maybe he could rescue the poor Scoper, before his jailers cured him of his soft and (sometimes) squeezable identity, his aptitude for hanging out and having fun, even in completely pointless, mindless circumstances.

What he almost certainly *couldn't* do, he realized, was head for home. No matter what his explanation was, his parents would make stupid jokes at his expense until/unless he bludgeoned them to death; worse yet, all his friends would think he was a wimp—especially Lisa and Roni. Not that they were all that special. But both of them had gotten wide-eyed hearing how he planned to make things happen instead of sitting home like everybody else and letting the same old crap just happen *to* them.

After a time, still very much awash in gloom, he roused himself and ate a cold and boring breakfast, thinking of the waffles that his mother might have made for him, back home, with melted butter puddled in their little indentations, and the honeypot at hand. And coffee, made with beans his father'd ground that very morning. He liked his waffles sweet enough to make his back teeth ache, washed down by one big mug of strong, black coffee.

When he'd finished eating, he attempted to convince himself he didn't have to go outside, that he could wait, hold out, until he stopped for gas, somewhere. But his insides forced their way into the argument and won, so he grabbed a jacket and his painter's cap and trudged into the woods. He'd had it up to here with No Facilities.

By the time he finally headed back toward the car, his mood absolutely matched the weather: foul. Now he knew that a rest stop in the woods, when it is raining really hard, is much, much, *much* more awkward and uncomfortable than one when it's dry. All he wanted was to get the hell away from where he was—this nowhere place—and totally erase all memory of ever having been there. Right away, at once, and fast. For the moment, what had happened in and by the brook the day before was gone, forgotten. He sloshed out of the woods and back up on the road. And very nearly panicked.

Through the blowing curtain of rain, he saw two figures by the car; one was standing and one was sitting. Both were facing him and looking back at him, but neither of them spoke. Both were super-saturated, totally sogged-out, hair plastered flat against their heads. Then the standing figure slowly raised its hand and brandished something at him . . . a sign! It told him Slow (although he'd stopped), and she was smiling. The sitting figure didn't move a muscle; its four big paws stayed firmly on the ground.

Phi started walking toward the pair, not fast. He hadn't been prepared for this; he'd convinced himself that she was history. While he tried to get his thoughts in order, he heard his mouth say, "Thea! God, you're soaked!" Not what you'd call profound, but accurate, at least. He'd been brought up to be a gentleman (of sorts) and *succor* (he believed the word was)

83

members of the weaker sex; reflexively, his hands came up and out, toward her. And, seeing that, she smiled. He totally ignored the other new arrival.

The dog, however, growled. The BIG DOG growled: a bass note, guttural and way back in its throat. Not so much "I'm going to kill and eat you, sucker, starting now," as "Watch it, kid, just watch it." Philo halted, dropped his hands down by his sides; on his face there grew an insincere and sappy smile.

The girl said, "Genie!" to the dog. "The mink is in the meadow. He's okay." The dog looked up at her and cocked its head, a question in its eyes.

"The *mink* is in the *meadow*," she repeated. "Drop."

The dog lay down and put its chin upon its forepaws, looking up at Phi. Raindrops splattered on its head; it didn't even blink. It was almost Great Dane size, but with a slightly different head, wide across the brow and floppy-eared, more like a leaner St. Bernard. Its coat was coarse and for the most part brown, or brownish gray. Right above its eyes, which were a lustrous chocolate color, its hair was darker, almost black.

"I'm sorry, Philo Fortune," Thea said to him. "Color me contemptible, a super-stinkeroo. *Scorn* me, even; you're entitled."

"What?" he said. This was all so . . . unexpected. *The mink is in the meadow?* What?

"I wasn't where I said I'd be, at six," she said. "I was getting *her*." She looked down at the dog. "Her name's Diogenes; Genie's short for that. You want to hear *amazing*? Her name *was* Genie, in her other life. Different spelling, with a *J,* but Genie."

"Diogenes?" said Philo stupidly. "Her other life?"

"She was in the CIA," said Thea. "And I had to get her when I did. It was a now-or-never type of deal. We walked all night to get here, though. Just on the

84

chance you'd be here. When I saw the car, I went bananas. Didn't I?" She squatted down to pat the big dog's head. "Virtue *is* its own reward, a lot of times."

Philo didn't know exactly what *he* felt like going. "Bananas" was too bland and everyday. He thought he might go passion fruit, or pomegranates. He was looking at the girl who'd caused him (in just two days' time) to act and feel a whole lot more *profoundly* and peculiarly than ever before in his life. And now she'd teamed up with a giant dog, who'd been in intelligence and, chances were, could kill with its bare paws.

"You want to hear this now?" said Thea, looking up at him. "What happened was, this woman I was sketching right around five-thirty, was the whole Humane Society of Garston. We started talking dogs, of course, as soon as I heard that."

"Don't tell me, let me guess. She had this . . . Genie, here, right back there in her shelter, I suppose," Philo managed to get out. "All ready for adoption."

"Exactly," Thea said. "Well, sort of. She's what they call a problem placement, on account of . . . well, her checkered past. Nobody seemed to want to take her on. They were at the point of . . . you know, putting her to sleep." Thea shook her head. "She's been deprogrammed, but . . . they *can* have flashbacks, apparently. So what the lady had to do was teach me all of Genie's special phrases, starting with the easygoing ones they didn't try to take away from her. Like 'the mink is in the meadow.' That means everything is cool and she can just relax."

While she was saying that, all that, Phi began to feel . . . a little nuts, standing in a downpour listening to . . . a dog's biography. But on the other hand (he told himself), his whole trip had been a little nuts, so far.

Maybe it'd be better if he simply tried to go with it, and not pass judgments on . . . himself, or anyone.

"You said she taught you *all* her special phrases, though?" he said, injecting interest in his voice, as water droplets fell from his nose. "Including any . . . bad ones?"

"Uh-huh." She nodded. "And of course that took a while. By then, of course, we'd met—Genie and I—and it was obvious the two of us were perfect for each other. But learning all I had to learn did take a bunch of time. The idea is, I have to be prepared in case somebody accidentally says one, ever, and she just . . . well, reacts. Not that that's too likely—either of those things. She's been deprogrammed, as I said, and they're not exactly usual, those phrases."

Philo also said "Uh-huh," while staring at the dog. He thought she looked a good deal wiser than he might have liked, more thoughtfully intelligent. He had a feeling he was being measured by the animal, sized up, right then. He felt that she was checking out his smarts and strength and, possibly, his loyalty, as well; his depth of feeling for the Constitution.

He also noticed that, by now, he was soaked through and through. He wanted to get in the car. In the past, he'd always had the sense to pass that simplest of IQ tests—to come in out of the rain. But still, he hesitated.

If he got in, Thea *and* the dog would almost surely get in, too. Was that okay with him? Having a dog with them, thus making "company" a "crowd"? A dog who'd already held a full-time job with the government and was, in that and other ways, superior to him?

In the end, the steady rain made up his mind to speak. That, and noticing how her wet shirt clung to Thea's body.

"Well, look," he said. "I guess we better get inside the car, get out of *here* and go on . . ."

". . . to a Laundromat," she finished for him, gaily. "What all of us—except for Genie—need is one big dryer." And she laughed. "Every stitch I own,"—she nodded at her purple duffel/laundry bag—"is *sloppo.*"

"Right," said Philo. As his mind lurched off in new directions, he was having trouble ordering his thoughts and taking charge. "Yes. Yes, good idea. Um, I suppose . . . well, if you wanted to, you two could hop in back. You and Genie, there. Good dog. And, well . . . I mean, that is, you could get into . . . . I mean *put on* some stuff, dry clothes, of *mine.* That's if you wanted to. I've got some, um, oh, some stuff like sweatpants in that suitcase, there, as well as other . . . stuff."

He guessed the trouble was that he hardly knew this girl. So while it was cool—considerate—to offer her dry clothes, it was also awkward to suggest that she strip right there, in front of him, or actually behind him, in the car. Yet, seeing as he'd already seen her totally undressed before . . .

"Great idea," he heard her saying. She moved around and lifted up the Squareback's big back door. "In fact, I think I'll take my wet stuff off out here, and wring it out before we're in the car. I can squeegee lots off Genie, too, I bet." And she started to undress, bent over, sheltered by the Skewbee's door.

Philo yanked the front door open, and squishily collapsed into the driver's seat, facing squarely front.

"Don't you want to do the same as me?" Her voice now came from right behind him, *in* the car. He heard the back door slam, the click of the dog's nails on the floor. With the backseat folded down, as it had been since he left home, there was *only* floor back there, and them, and luggage.

87

She laughed. "You ought to move into the other seat," she said. "It's a whole lot easier undressing there,"—she laughed again—"as you may know."

Feeling, well, a little challenged, Phi moved, crab-like, to his right and started to take off his clothes. He realized that pretty soon, and for the first time in his life, he would be naked, with a naked (?) girl, inside a car. Wasn't that the hope, the dream, of every boy his age in the entire Western world? Wouldn't Eddie bust a gut if he could see his buddy, stripping down, not even looking at the girl, and being eyeballed by a killer dog?

No sooner had he gotten off his final article of clothing—a pair of sporty low-rise briefs—than a towel came sailing from the back and landed on his knee. Good grief, he thought; she's watching me. He started drying off as best he could; the towel was damp already and smelled just a little bit of dog. Next on his agenda: turning all the way around to get dry clothes.

He bit his lip. "You decent?" he called out, dredging up his mother's homespun line.

Thea answered what he heard as "Yup." He did a rapid spin and faced her, kneeling on the seat.

Except she'd probably said "Huh?" She, too, was kneeling, still digging in his suitcase, and altogether nude. Botticelli could have done her: *Venus in the Squareback.*

"I guess I'll pass on underwear and just wear these," she said to him, holding up his dark blue sweats. "Okay?"

Once again, she didn't seem upset at all by being seen . . . that way. For his part, Philo pressed his lower front against the seat back and found he couldn't take a real deep breath.

"Well," she said. She seemed amused by his discomfiture. She yanked his sweatshirt overhead, and started pulling on the pants. He, meanwhile, went head down inside the suitcase, grabbing underwear, a pair of shorts, a polo shirt, his running shoes.

"You really have a nice physique," she said. "What were you, Mr. Varsity, back home?"

"No, no," he muttered, dressing fast. "I'm not into that . . . mentality at all." He made himself calm down, relax. "I ride my bike and have a weight set, though." He now was fully dressed again, and thinking. There was *stuff* he now could say.

He cleared his throat. "But speaking of physiques," he said, "I meant to tell you this before. *You* look to be in some *fantastic* shape; you're . . . *beautiful!*"

He was careful not to turn around while saying that; if she went puke-faced from the compliment, he didn't want to know it. Instead, he picked the towel back up and dried the driver's seat.

"I live a pretty strenuous existence," she replied. "I do that 'cause it's good for me, that's all. It's part of self-sufficiency, being in the best shape possible. It makes me less dependent, more capable of taking care of Thea. I know a lot of ways to hurt someone, but how *I* feel is what I care about. What other people think is no concern of mine."

She hadn't sounded flattered *or* offended—just off-hand and impersonal, as usual; nothing seemed to touch her or excite her much—except for maybe dogs and nature—and probably her own ideas.

Philo switched back to the driver's seat and turned around to look at her.

Now she was sitting on the floor, leaning against the side of the car, with the dog's big head in her lap. She looked relaxed and pleasant, very much at home, neither liking nor disliking him, he thought. His sweatsuit was much too big for her, but she looked . . . cute in it, to him.

"How about you hand your wet clothes back?" she said to him. "And that towel up there. I've made a pile of all my stuff." She gestured toward the soggy heap by the big back door.

He did as she suggested.

"You want to sit up here, or what?" he said. "I guess we're set to go."

"No, this is fine," she said. "I'll keep Genie company, for now." She sounded serious, but not dismissive. "The two of us are bonding still, you know."

As it turned out, no one got to do much bonding in the time it took to find a Laundromat. There was one right smack dab on the highway, not more than half a mile from where it met the country road.

They had the place all to themselves, when the three of them walked in, two with armloads of wet clothing. Thea and the dog were barefoot still, and one of them had a wallet in her mouth.

"Let's not argue; this hot air's on me," said Thea when they'd dumped their stuff into two dryers and the dog had dropped the wallet on the floor in front of her.

She took out a bill and fed it into a slot that turned it into quarters. She stuck those into both machines.

"Let's watch," she said, and sat down on an orange plastic chair, one of a row that faced the dryers. The dog flopped down in front of her.

"It's kind of soothing, don't you think?" said Thea, staring. "I've fallen fast asleep in front of dryers. Or, hey,"—she tore her eyes away, looked up at Phi—"d'you suppose that I was hypnotized? And never even knew it?" She giggled. "Maybe I went out and got a garden hose and sprayed . . . oh, a parade, or everybody in a restaurant. I could have done the dryer's bidding. *Maytag* made me do it; Maytag, ruler of the planet Calgon. Doesn't that sound *Star Trek*-y?"

Philo smiled and nodded, shrugged. He couldn't quite believe he was about to watch some laundry dry, for fun. He looked down at the dog, then at the chair beside the girl. The dog looked up at him and nodded, so he sat. It would be nice, he thought, if someone in their group would get the urge to bond with *him.*

"I also want to give you money for the car, the gas," she said, opening her wallet once again.

"Oh, that's all right," he said, but without a lot of heart in it.

"I insist," said Theodora. "I made a *fortune,* yesterday; you must have picked the perfect spot to let me off. I tried to give the Genie lady all of what I had. She took a few, but look how much she didn't take. So, here."

She pushed a wad of bills at him. It looked to Phi as if her stash was ones and fives, exclusively, but there were quite a few of them. He thought they could add up to fifty, sixty bucks, or more. He could feed the Squareback gas for weeks with that much money. Was this a sidekick sent from heaven—bearing all the cash he hadn't even tried to sweet-talk from his mother?

"No, really," he said lamely, one last time.

"*Philo Fortune.*" Thea sounded almost cross. The dog looked up. "Let's not be difficult, all right? I don't *want* this junk. I told you that before. Money makes me . . . let's just say uncomfortable." She smiled. "You, however, don't mind having it. So you should be the keeper of the cash. Unless, of course—," she looked around; her eyes fell on a big green trash can, "you'd rather I just . . ."

"No, no, no," he said sincerely, following her glance.

"That won't be necessary." He took the money, but he made a show of holding it loosely before he shoved it carelessly—offhandedly—into the pocket of his shirt.

"Thanks, Mom," he said, with just a little laugh. She didn't even ask him what he meant by that.

One thing about a dryer: it gets clothes dry. Philo already had that fact at his command. He also knew that when a person's clothes are dry, someone (as a rule, his mother) folds them up (and often puts them in his room) and then moves on to doing something else.

In this case, he and Thea both did the folding. Which meant it soon was time for something else.

"Well," she said, facing both that fact and him. "Now what? Have we gotten to the moment in the script where we shake hands and say good-bye, good luck— and maybe *think*, good riddance?"

The question sort of jarred him. Stupidly (he thought) he hadn't seen it coming. He'd more or less assumed that they'd . . . continue on together. He'd thought she wanted to do that and he knew *he* did. At some point—though he couldn't pinpoint when—the main . . . well, goal or *purpose* of this trip had shifted, slightly. Now what he wanted most was just to get a better bead on *Thea*.

With this question, though, he had to wonder. Was he at the point of being dumped? If so, he sure as hell would want to dump her first.

"Good question," he replied. He looked outside; it still was raining hard. A pickup with two women in it was just pulling in beside the S-back. "And to further complicate the situation, there's the fact I haven't really thought about exactly where I plan to go from here. I mean, it might be Timmonsville." He watched the women open up the pickup's cap and drag two laundry baskets out, both full to overflowing. "Or Dog-

92

gett possibly, or maybe I'll veer south a ways." The women clomped into the Laundromat.

"Uh-huh," said Thea noncommittally.

"He don't allow no dogs in here," said one of the new arrivals, looking unenthusiastically at Genie. She was skinny, with her hair in white curlers under a plastic rain hat. On her pink sweatshirt were the words "Tough Noogies."

Philo welcomed the diversion. "It's okay," he said. "This dog's in training for the Seeing Eye. As a guide dog for the blind? We have to get her used to all the places she might have to go in, when she gets an owner. She's been learning which machines are which in here, and all."

"Is that the truth?" the woman said, but not suspiciously. "I'd heard them dogs are really smart."

"Absolutely," Philo said. "Once you show 'em how to do a thing, they're aces at it."

"Well, I oughta get one for my daughter," the other woman said. "The way her wash comes out."

"Come on, Jennifer," Philo said to Thea. "Time to take Melissa to the supermarket." And picking up both stacks of folded clothes, he headed for the door.

Outside, Thea said, "What? *Jennifer? Melissa?* Why not Brandi?" She let out a laugh. It sounded like a friendly—and companionable—one.

"I never give real names to strangers," Philo said, flashing a swift smile that could have been a grimace or a gas pain. He stood there, looking at the car; the girl and the dog stood there beside him, also looking at the car.

Nobody moved. The question Thea'd asked still floated in the air, between them. Damn it, Philo thought, I should have asked it first. He took a deep, deep breath.

"So, what're you waiting for?" he said. "Hop in."

93

"Hop in?" she echoed. "You mean you want us to go *with* you, wherever you decide to go? Better think it over one more time. You sure? Or wait. Is it just you want me to get in and change, so I can give you back your sweats?"

He didn't answer, hoping she'd figure that she had to get in either way; then he could simply follow, start the car, and drive.

"Which one is it, Philo Fortune? Or whatever your name is," Thea said.

"Iwantyoubothtocomewithme," said Philo with his head down, stepping out into the rain, opening his door, and piling in, the stacks of clothes now tumbled in his lap. She'd made him, gotten him, to say it. Now it wasn't she who had agreed to come with him; he'd *asked* her to.

Through the rain-streaked windshield, he saw the girl bend over and say something, softly, to the dog. The dog looked over at the car, then back at her. There was a pause, then matching nods; Genie rose and trotted toward the back door of the Squareback. Thea ran and let her in and piled in after her. Philo smelled the now-familiar wet-dog smell. He sighed and turned the key in the ignition.

As Philo drove along, the steady rain became a little play-
ful, turned into a drizzle. In the direction they were
traveling, west, the sky got lighter and broke into a
few huge mounds of shadowed clouds; all of a sudden, distant hills were visible.

And as that happened, Phi believed he felt a different atmosphere inside the car, as well. At first, that
was a hard thing to account for. Thea hadn't climbed
into the seat beside him, whimpering with pleasure.
She and her enormous dog still sat and lay on his
foam pad, which she'd unrolled on the floor, in back.
So, in terms of pure geography, she remained about
as far away from him as she could get while still staying in the vehicle.

But nonetheless, she felt less *separate* to him; indeed, it seemed they were *together* in the car. There
wasn't any of the sort of strangeness, even nervousness, he'd felt back home, the few times he'd
picked up an unknown person, hitching. As they
rolled along, he chatted easily about the fast-improv-
ing weather, and the scenery, and the different kinds

of cars he thought he'd like to have someday, and how much better back roads were than driving on the interstates.

He decided that the different feeling in the car was due to *her* being different; he didn't think he'd changed that much. But there was now no longer any question about his having changed *some.* He'd very recently admitted, quite out loud and not just to himself, that he . . . well, sort of needed someone, her, to be with him. And it had been a different kind of needing than the way he'd needed Eddie on this trip. And although there wasn't any doubt he (also) wanted her (the way he wanted all attractive members of her gender), there was more (a good deal more) than lust involved in this. In some peculiar way he couldn't understand at all, Thea (just the way she was) was forcing him to redefine himself. In part, perhaps, so he could let her know, somehow, exactly who he was— for instance, someone she could *like,* even admire.

Once she'd had more time with him, perhaps she'd see he wasn't quite so much her opposite as she'd first thought. Perhaps already she had seen him in a slightly different light. *He'd* been where he'd said he'd be at six o'clock the day before. And then he'd even gone the extra mile: returned to where she said she'd like to spend a second night. If those were not two solid shows of virtue, well, he didn't know what would be.

She'd also come right out and said he had a nice physique, and while that wasn't exactly a proposition, it told him she was looking at—and, yes, respecting— him.

No, it was pretty clear she didn't find it painful, being in his presence.

He thought perhaps he'd now move on and cultivate the dog. That absolutely couldn't hurt, either way you looked at it. After all, it was the truth; he *did* like dogs.

A sign said Timmonsville—160.

"Yo," said Phi. "Timmonsville, one-sixty. How's about a college tour? It's on my Doubtful list, but still."

"College?" Thea said.

"Genie'd meet some interesting dogs, I'll bet. One thing I've learned about a college campus: always lotsa dogs around."

"Timmonsville's a *college?*" Thea asked.

"Not Timmonsville," said Phi. "But just beyond it, in the town of Riddle. Riddle University. The Sphinxes."

"What?" she said. "The *what?* Is that where everybody meditates?"

"*Meditates?*" said Phi. He couldn't help but curl a lip around the word. "No, of course it isn't. Not so far as *I* know, anyway." Now, *masturbates,* he thought, might be more like it, what with people getting so afraid of AIDS and all.

"You know the one I mean, though," Thea said. "They want to bring about world peace that way, everybody doing it? I meditate, sometimes. But I'd never do it in a group. That, or anything else, I guess."

"Riddle has a real good business program, I believe," Phi said, in part to get his mind off everybody "doing it."

"What?" said Thea. "How about you? You ever meditate?"

Philo sighed, run over, flattened by her train of thought. "Nah," he said. "I'm pretty sure it wouldn't work for me. I'm looking for *ideas,* not different ways to make my mind go blank. I don't believe in pyramids or crystals, either. Any of that crap."

"I see," said Thea, and then, barely audibly, "clink-a-tinkle-dink."

Philo only raised his eyebrows, letting whatever *that*

meant pass. "I'm more the Genie type," he said. "If I can't see it, sniff it, lick it, scratch it, it's not there, as far as I'm concerned."

"Right. Uh-huh," she said. He thought he heard a smile in there.

A few miles farther on, they hit a bump, and Philo heard a little sound, like "clink-a-tinkle-dink." It was made, he realized, by all his other keys that hung below the one in the ignition, hitting up against the silver medal on his key ring. The one that said Saint Christopher, protect us.

"You're going to go to college, then," said Thea. "Somewhere, sometime."

They'd stopped for gas, and Philo was self-serving. Thea'd gotten out to watch the process. The rain had stopped half an hour earlier, and it was muggy out.

"I guess," said Philo, ever wary of the c word (which was *commitment,* still). "It's a crapshoot, though—the choosing part." The Squareback's gas tank was up front. You could hear the gas slosh back and forth, sometimes, if you were sitting in one of the two front seats. Not a real romantic thing to listen to, Phi had always felt.

"So I've heard," she said. "I've heard it gives kids nervous breakdowns, getting shot down by a bunch of colleges for no good reason. It's kind of like 'She loves me; she loves me not,' I guess—you know, the flower petal game." She was standing looking at the car straight on. "You want me to clean the windshield?"

"Sure," he said, and watched her go and lift the scrubber-squeegee thing out of a pail of ancient-looking water. "It isn't all that bad, but sure."

"I'd hate to get rejected by some idiot," she said,

scrubbing at the few small smears left on the glass by head-ons with the summer insect population.

"That's not what I meant," he said. "I meant *my* choosing where I'd want to go, which ones. You can really screw yourself, you know."

"You can?" she said. She'd rinsed the tool and turned it over, now was squeegeeing the surface clean. She did a perfect job, he noticed; the windshield now was spotless, streakless—perfect.

"I thought everybody knew the best ones," she continued. "Stanford. MIT. Like that."

Phi had changed to watching the gauges on the gas pump. When pumping gas, he liked to go full speed and then release the handle suddenly, and have the $ gauge stop on however-many dollars and zero-zero cents. That was pretty near impossible to do, and so he made a rule that five cents either way was lucky. This time, he hit $8.01, and that was excellent—a harbinger (he felt) of more good things to come.

"That's the way it used to be," he said to Thea as he shoved the nozzle up into its holster in the gas pump. "Back in my father's day." He reached into the pocket of his shirt. "These days, it isn't quite so simple."

She walked along with him as he went to pay.

The kid behind the counter looked a little bit like Christian Slater—but with a different dental plan.

"Eight-oh-one on the regular?" he said. He looked at Phi and then at Thea, longer, and then once again at Phi. Then he picked up a penny from the little plastic tray atop his register. "Let's say eight dollars, even."

Phi handed him three singles and a five. He was sure the guy was envious of him.

"Thank you very much and have a real nice day," the guy then said, and snuck another peek at Thea's chest.

"I hope that you do, too," said Philo, with a tolerant, good-winner's smile.

Genie was standing up when they approached the car again. As soon as she saw Thea, she began to wag her tail.

"Maybe I ought to take her for a little walk, if that's all right with you." The girl looked up at Philo. "Let her stretch her legs and pee."

"Sure," he said. "Of course." He gave the dog a scratch behind one ear as she got out. "The mink is in the meadow," he said, and the dog looked up at him, approvingly, he thought. "I'll just move the car out of the way," he said to Thea.

She nodded, reached inside the car, and grabbed her leash, then got it on the big dog's collar. The Christian Slater–looking guy was standing in the station door, now, smiling, looking at both Genie and the girl. Philo heard him say, "What kinda dog is that one, anyway? He sure is *big,* all right."

After he'd parked the car out of the way, Phi took his mother's little whisk broom from the glove compartment and brushed some leaves and dirt out of the Squareback's back. He didn't even bother making sure that Thea saw what he was doing.

"So, getting back to what you started telling me," she said. They were once again inside the car, same places as before. He felt the atmosphere was now, if anything, still better. "You were saying colleges have different reputations, year to year?"

"Not always, but a lot of times," he said. "Like other products, colleges get hot—in different ways, for different reasons. Also, programs can cool off if certain teachers leave, for instance, or if they change requirements, or offerings. Word gets around."

"It sounds like what you're looking for is mostly a—

what was it that you said?—*credential,* then," said Thea. "Another thing that might impress somebody else."

"If you want to put it that way—yes," said Phi. He felt the caution flag go up. "But that's what everybody's doing." Weak, perhaps, but true.

"But how about the person getting the credential—say, yourself? Is all this going to make you happy?"

Phi made a quickie puke-face, but then, as quickly, changed it to a smile. Everybody seemed to have a "happy" question for him.

"Shucks," he said, "who knows? Sometimes I think that happy's like a fall-back school, a place you kind of settle for, you know? When you find out you haven't made the bigs."

He glanced into the rearview mirror, fixed it so that he could look at her. He wished he could take back what he'd just said. It was the sort of thing he said at school, sometimes, more for effect than anything.

It was hard to tell what she was thinking, with her head turned slightly, looking out the window.

"But how about yourself and education?" He stuck that in there fast and re-aimed the mirror toward the traffic coming from behind. "Does it have a place in your . . . well, lifestyle?"

"I don't know," she said. "I kind of doubt it. I couldn't stand the self-indulgent preppy little toy chests I went to high school with. The way I figure, college might be worse. Except there *is* a possibility . . . oh, I don't know."

"Of what?" he said. "What possibility?"

"Well, I think I'd like to take a little—*I* don't know, don't laugh—philosophy," she said. "I think."

"Philosophy," said Phi, without inflection. He knew the meaning of the word: essentially, the study of profound and boring things like ethics, metaphysics, and a lot of other useless drivel. He'd learned the names of some philosophers in high school courses that he'd had to take, and even read brief excerpts from the works of one or two—like Mill, for instance. And he'd seen Department of Philosophy in college catalogs, which meant there were whole *courses* offered in the stuff.

"Yes," she said. "I've learned already that there's one that suits me fine. Maybe there are others I'd like even more."

"Wait," he said. Up to this point, he had thought of her as being pretty much a cool, fast-flowing stream, but quite a shallow one. Now, a *philosophy* "that suits me fine"—was this some unexpected depth or just a shadow?

"You're into a philosophy?" he said. "Which one?"

"Cynicism," Thea said. She shrugged. "A guidance person at my high school turned me on to it. Not on purpose, though. He thought he was insulting me."

"I don't get it," Philo said.

"He didn't like my attitude," she said. "He told me I was rude and inconsiderate of fellow students. He said my reputation in the high school stank, and that I didn't even seem to care. He asked me what I had to say for myself. But before I got a word out, he said, 'And don't bother to tell me that you're merely model-ing yourself on old Diogenes of Sinope.' Which natu-rally intrigued me, even though I knew the guy was only showing off."

"Diogenes of Sinope?" Philo said. (The name Dioge-nes, which rang faint bells for him, was clearly some-thing major in her life.) He wasn't wild about the prog-ress of this conversation. It was making him feel nervous, insecure. But he also wondered if it might be . . . oh, a crazy kind of *foreplay,* perhaps the open sesame to ever knowing Thea, either biblically or so-cially.

"Yes, you've heard of him, I'm sure," she said. "Follower of Socrates, 412 (question mark) to 323 B.C., lived in a tub and all that jazz? Told Alexander of Macedon to get out of his light, supposedly; roamed all over looking for 'a man'? Some say 'an honest man,' but I don't think that's right; and, personally, I have my doubts he even owned a lantern. He—and most of the other Cynics—they were into poverty and self-sufficiency. They didn't give a shit what anybody thought—probably some of them really stank—and they weren't into formal education or politics, both of which they thought were bull, I guess. Their basic *thing* was what I told you earlier: that virtue, which is shown by deeds and by living as simply as possible (the way a dog does), is the only good. Period." She paused. "That's it. I've yapped too much, I think. You asked; I told you. Now I'd like to just shut up a while."

It seemed to Philo that he had two choices at that point. One, pay no attention to her likes and dislikes, argue, show her (get her to admit) that what she'd said was stupid (even more so in this day and age); that would have been his typical response. Or, two, shut up, as she'd just said she wanted to.

It was a perfect Lady or the Tiger sort of deal, he thought.

In the studio inside his mind, the audience cried out, "Number one! Choose number one!" But in a back row sat his mother with two fingers up.

Hmm, he thought. And then: Why, after all, did Thea have to think this way or that? Why *shouldn't* she believe exactly as she said she did—*and* have a little quiet when she wanted it? His parents didn't tell each other what to think or do and got along just great.

He found that he was nodding as he drove along in silence.

"You ought to pick her up," said Thea, from the back.

No doubt she was referring to the person on the shoulder of the road, ahead, just past the exit from the Taco Bell: the hitchhiker. Even as the words came out of Thea's mouth, Philo was wondering, Would it be cool to pick her up—or not?

The hitchhiker was a *her* all right, even from a distance. No guy would wear such big, wide khaki shorts, that kind of round straw hat. And even if a guy put on a sleeveless top—pink and oversized—it wouldn't hang on him that way.

Philo brought the Squareback to a stop beside her.

She grabbed the handle of the door but didn't open it at once. Instead, she looked inside, at him, and then in back—saw Thea and the dog, and smiled.

"Thank God." As she got in, she also chuckled. She looked to Philo like she was the sort who's used to taking cabs, to being in control. He kind of liked that quality, though mostly in a guy. "Up to now, I thought there must have been a jailbreak somewhere. Every guy that stopped was adenoidal and had multiple tattoos. I swear I got to feeling like a two-days'-dead impala at the jackals' lodge night."

She tossed most of that at Thea, in the back, but Philo wasn't totally left out. As soon as she got in, she bent both legs and put her sandaled feet up on the dashboard. The bottoms of the big, wide shorts, impelled by gravity, slid down her bare tan legs right to the car seat, exposing one of them to him—its outside, anyway—up to the bottom of her smoothly rounded rear.

Phi took some deep breaths through his nose.

"So what's your destination?" he inquired.

"Timmonsville," she said. "Or, really, three-point-two miles farther down the road. But Timmonsville would be fantastic, if you're going there—that far."

"Your fantasy's fulfilled," said Philo, smoothly. "You've caught the Timmonsville Express."

"I'm Thea," Thea said. "This gorgeous creature on my lap is Genie. Our pilot says his name is Captain Philo."

"Tanya," said the girl, swiveling and shaking hands with Thea. "This is great. I feel so lucky that you stopped. I've never met a Philo in the flesh, before." She cocked her head at him.

"Nor I a Tanya," Philo countered, with just an eye flick back at her bare haunch. "You're not, by any chance, a Riddle student, are you?" Though he was sure that she was older, he was still the *guy.*

"Why, yes, by some unlikely chance I am," she said. "Just for this one summer, though. And since of course you're wondering,"—she gave another little laugh and tossed her head again, toward Thea—"the answer's no, I'm not."

"Not what?" asked Thea, cheerfully confused.

"Not making up the courses that I flunked the spring semester," Tanya said, "down at NYU, where I belong.

I'm at Riddle buying me some extra credits, so I graduate ahead of time—like this December. I wanted easy little bullshit courses and a pleasant country campus. How could I go wrong at Riddle?"

"I never thought you'd *flunked*," said Thea, ingenuously. "You don't look to be the type at all."

Philo had to go along with that. The girl had "winner" written everywhere on her, all over—on her clothes and legs and way of speaking. Tanya, clearly, wasn't any patsy.

Now she laughed her easy laugh again. "Because my hairline doesn't meet my eyebrows? Hey, you never know." She ran both hands along one smooth, smooth leg. "They make some great depilatories, nowadays. But actually,"—she sobered up—"you're right. I'm pretty anal, when it comes to facts; I eat up tests and stuff. We all do, all of us accounting majors. The only way I'm different from the rest of them is I'll be out there looking for a job while they're still dirty, rotten schoolboys." And she rolled her eyes at Philo, making it quite clear to him she knew that she was different from the rest of them in other ways, as well.

Phi cleared his throat. "I'm curious," he said. "You hear so many different stories. Aside from the sorts of courses that you chose, what's the word on Riddle? Is it any good?"

"Good?" she said. "I suppose it all depends on what you mean by 'good.' Practically speaking, it's just about a total waste of time."

"You mean, in terms of learning any *skills,* or going on to decent *jobs,* or what?" asked Phi. He'd always been impressed by Riddle's reputation.

"All of the above," said Tanya, with a wave. "Far as I can see, Riddle students get no training whatsoever. They used to do a decent job in business ed and econ, but no more. Today, the Sphinxes can't *do* anything, except the Sunday crossword in the *New York Times.* I suppose they—some of them—end up professors or philosophers. Or they write some sort of book or something." She brushed a wisp of honey-colored hair back under her straw hat.

Phi knew his mother would have liked that thumbnail sketch of Riddle education; she would have sent away for application forms for him in no time flat. But he wondered how his passenger/philosopher had handled what this down-to-earth accounting major'd said.

He was not about to turn his head around and look at her, just then. He'd started to, but then, from the corner of his eye, he'd got (instead) a glimpse of part of Tanya's bare left breast, seen through the spacious armhole of her big pink top while that one arm was raised.

"But you," he croaked at her, "you'll be all set. Everybody always needs a good accountant. And graduating early'll mean that you can pick and choose, I'll bet."

"Right," said Tanya. *"Sure."* And, "Don't I wish." She sounded agitated. "Good jobs are few and far between, these days—even in accounting. They say a quarter of my class won't even find work in the field. And being female is a handicap, of course. Chances are I'll end up waiting tables, or receptionist-ing . . ." Now she was doing something with her legs that Philo'd never seen—or heard—a person do, before: hitting her knees together in a way that made the soft flesh of her inner thighs produce a kind of thwacking as it collided with . . . itself. "And living in my parents' house again."

For a moment, there was no sound in the car, other than that rhythmic thwacking sound.

"Are people going into the Peace Corps, still?" asked Thea, from the back.

"I guess, a few," said Tanya. And she stopped that nervous knee-thing. "People on the fringe. The tree-huggers—*you* know. Me, I don't think I've got the right to waltz into a Third World country and start telling someone else what they should do. How could *I* know, really? Plus, I can't quite see me out there, planting maize. I mean, can you?"

Thinking that she might be asking him that question, Philo shook his head a little. As he did so, Tanya took her left foot off the dashboard and crossed it over her right knee, affording him the chance to run his eyes along that left leg's inner surfaces, noisy thigh included. He tried to think if it was maize that women planted bare-shanked, standing in the water.

"You know what *I* wish, Cap'n Philo?" Tanya said. Clearly this—the next thing that she said—was just for him. She was even looking straight at him, and steadily, and not at Thea. He sort of braced himself. "I wish, sometimes, that I was in my fifties, now. I'd like to be my parents."

"Your *parents*?" Philo yelped reflexively. "Hey, you're kidding, right? You wouldn't want to be your parents! *Would* you?"

"All right, in certain ways I wouldn't, no." Tanya sounded sulky, saying that. "I'd miss out on a lot of . . . well, excitement. But they never had to worry. It just isn't fair; things were better, back when they were my age. They could do exactly what they wanted to—go out, work hard, and just relax. Knowing by the time they got to fifty, they'd be sitting pretty. They've gotten everything they want. Who knows if I ever will?"

"Well, lots of people do," said Philo. "That's the way I look at it. Somebody almost always hits the number, right? And so it might as well be me as anybody else. Or you," he thought to add. "Or Thea."

"Sure," said Thea, from the back. "Or Thea."

He drove the Squareback all the way to Riddle U, to Tanya's dorm, where she'd slip on a bathing suit, she said, and go and stretch out by the pool.

After she was gone, Philo took a little time to get his thoughts together. Then he turned around and scowled.

"Wasn't that incredible?" he said. "Her wishing she was fifty? God, you'd think a business or accounting major'd want to—"

At that point, Thea cut him off, however.

"But *you'd* have liked to do some business with . . . well, *her,* now wouldn't you?" she said. "She really turned you on—and now, alas, she's gone." She made a little clucking sound. "But all need not be lost; you could hit the number still. How's about *we* take a motel room, you and *me*—in lieu of Tanya. Who knows? You might have lots of fun." She laughed. "As long as Genie doesn't think you're hurting me."

She chose the place, Jomar's Motel. It was small and old with gray asbestos shingles all along the front of it and no cars parked by any of the units. A neon sign confirmed that there was still a Vacancy.

"We're looking for a hurter," Thea'd said before they found it. "All the chains—Best Western and them—they'd tell us to get lost. Motel 6'd turn out the lights if we pulled up, I bet." She laughed. "The Lord and Lady Smith, with Princess Genie." And she laughed again, but maybe not wholeheartedly.

Phi'd nodded, going right along with it, and trying to look . . . oh, lecherous and mischievous. That wasn't easy as the normal wetness from the inside of his mouth began to move, as if by magic, to the surface of his palms.

For a while, he'd thought that this was her idea of fun—a little joke—and so he'd "Sure, why not?"-ed everything she said, acting like this kind of thing was ordinary pepperoni on the pizza of his life. But when he saw that she was serious about their getting a motel room, having sex—and *now*—that was the moment he got really nervous. It was as if he, once again, was walking up the sidewalk toward School, on the day he really *had to* go to kindergarten. Fantasy was one thing. Imagining yourself in bed with someone that you knew was cinchy—even kind of fun. But real life was an altogether different matter. So, sure, he'd put a condom on that once, but never in his life in front of *strangers.*

He never thought that he'd be losing his virginity with someone who he'd never kidded with, or kissed. Of course he'd heard kids talk about their one-night stands, and how they'd done it on first dates, but he'd been unimpressed. That wasn't how a smart guy played the game these days. But even putting danger to one side, he'd been convinced there was a better way.

That had happened just two years before, at what his dad had called their Swear-to-God Last Sex Talk. In fact, his *mom* was the main speaker. Phi thought she might have been a little buzzed, or stoned. She'd looked real dreamy-eyed and used a lot of slang without embarrassment. She'd told him sex, the act itself, was "the spire of a great cathedral"—which meant its height depended on the stuff beneath it, both the size and strength of it, and the space and time it took to put it all together. *He'd* been a bit embarrassed, listening to her, at first, but the longer she went on, the more he thought he "got it," the more he thought he (maybe) saw the way sex was from her perspective, as a female. And afterward, he thought about it more and came to feel that what she'd said made sense for *anyone* and was in fact real beautiful. That it was something he could buy, believe in. And he did.

But now? Thea volunteered to check them in, if he'd give her back some cash. "I'll be believable," she said. "Only a *wife*'d wear her husband's baggy sweatsuit." She grinned at him. "You can do the luggage, dear. If we show we've brought a lot of clothes and stuff, that'll make us even more authentic. They'll think we're honeymooners, maybe." She had her purple baseball cap back on again.

Philo nodded, very much relieved. He'd been dreading checking in, writing maybe Ed and Brandi Skiles. But as soon as she disappeared inside the office, he ran across the street and—yes!—there *was* a guy bee-lining for South End Liquors, and he looked perfect. He had a fat gut hanging out of a work shirt and shades on and a lunch box, and an enormous head of hair and matching mustache. Not a goody-goody kind of guy at all, much more the type who'd "been a kid once, too." He took the five Phi handed him and came out minutes later with his six-pack and a pint of vodka in a small brown bag.

"Just right," the big guy said, and winked, "with my commission in there." And he passed the bottle over, but no change.

Phi recrossed the street, put quarters in the soda machine, and won himself a can of Sprite. Then he started pulling luggage past the dog and out onto the walk—just as Thea exited the office, holding up the key to Unit 5, making it swing back and forth, as if it were a school (or dinner) bell.

He thought the room looked perfect for the part it had to play: crummy flop, out on the edge of town.

The walls were fake wood paneling and on them hung some smudgy prints depicting pink and white and purple flowers in a terra-cotta vase. There was just the one double bed with a chenille bedspread, a luggage rack, an upholstered maple armchair, and a writing table with a straight-back maple chair in front of it.

The TV was on a little wheeled cart, and there was a stain on the brown tweed rug right by the bedside table; the mirror, looking a little old and lined, was set into the bathroom door.

The bathroom sink and toilet both were pink, and the wall behind the toilet was missing a few tiles. There wasn't any tub, just a tiny shower stall. But there were two glasses in cellophane on the shelf by the sink, and at least four folded towels on racks, and the place smelled clean.

Phi set Thea's case and laundry bag beside his suitcase and his backpack, by the door. He didn't know if she expected they would stay the night; it was only 5 P.M.

The first thing Thea did was choose a spot for Genie on the floor, right in the corner by the bathroom door. While Philo stood and watched she grabbed a towel, got down on her hands and knees, and made the dog lie down on it. Eventually, she stood back up again and smiled at *him.*

"Ah," she said, "our little love nest. Be right out." With that she disappeared into the bathroom, closed the door. In a bit, he heard the toilet flush and water running.

To pass the time, Phi worked the pop-top on the soda can and loosened the cap on the vodka bottle without taking it off. He was waiting to get at the glasses in the bathroom and maybe borrow the key from her so he could hunt up some ice. Drinking alcohol was not a thing he liked to do, but he knew that in the short term, anyway, a drink would make him more relaxed and . . . carefree.

He looked over when he heard the bathroom door open. "You got the—?" he started but went no further. He could see she didn't have the key on her, not anymore. She'd undressed in the bathroom—typically, completely. She went directly to the bed, pulled the spread and bedclothes down, and flopped onto her back. Only then, as she arranged a pair of pillows underneath her head, did she . . . acknowledge he was part of this.

"Come on, slowpoke. Whatcha waitin' for?" she said. She took a breath, and stretched both arms straight out, and beckoned with her pointer fingers. The gesture didn't look . . . authentic. It seemed like something from a high school play.

But he knew *his* role demanded he look eager, so he took his clothes off quickly, lobbing them onto the maple armchair. Then he noticed that he still had on his running shoes, and so he yanked them off, too, while thinking: *There.* It wasn't like undressing by the brook, the day before. This was more like at the doctor's, for a physical.

"Oh, my, that's better," Thea said. "Now come to Mama." Her voice seemed different, too.

"Right," he grunted, as he made an awkward head-first dive onto the bed, beside her. Lacking any script, he put his arms around her upper back and started kissing her. At first his head was full of "here I go" and "wonder if . . . ," but in a little while it was as if his nervousness got stirred into the thick, hot pleasure of the moment, where it wholly disappeared.

Before he knew it, he was saying (and believing), "Thea, darling—gosh—I *love* you."

Time passed. The kissing and all that continued. It was the best that Philo'd ever had. Not having any clothing that he had to pull out or undo, or work his way around or under . . . that made things so much smoother, better. Every part of her he touched excited him. "Oh, Thea," he repeated and repeated, "you're *so* beautiful."

He couldn't help but be aware—*become* aware—of how his body was behaving: normally, thank God, just the way it always did when he was doing stuff with girls. Clearly, it did not discriminate on grounds of no past history; it had risen to the challenge. Now the only question was . . . but then, at that point, *she* appeared to notice that his body was behaving normally, and that discovery, apparently, excited or intrigued her. (Think of a Christmas morning scene, perhaps some years ago, when you found out that what was in that box *was* Super Mario. What did you do then? Of course. She did the same.)

Nothing wrong with that, except . . . that well before it crossed Phi's mind to go and get his condoms (which were deep inside his backpack by the door), there suddenly became no pressing need for them, and Thea, possibly surprised (and disappointed?), giggled (out of nervousness, amusement, or disgust?) and marveled (maybe), "Well . . . !" She pulled the top sheet partway up and did a little mopping.

This largely unexpected and unwelcome happening sent Philo through the mood swing of his life. From bouncing on the bungee cord of ecstasy, he dropped into the swamp of black despair. And once he started wallowing, he had no past, no memories of soaring. All he knew was present time, humiliation—and, of course, the loathsome name for what had happened.

"Mmm—*damn!*" he said, facedown on the bed; his hands, no longer touching her, were fists beneath his chest.

She didn't speak, so in a little while, he rolled away from her and off the bed, where, standing, he collected his undershorts and put them on. Then he headed for the bathroom, where he grabbed a water glass. When he looked up from pouring vodka for himself, and Sprite, he saw she'd pulled the bedclothes up, right to her chin.

"None for me?" she said.

"You want some?" That was a surprise.

"Sure," she said. "Why not? It isn't every day . . ."

He went and got the other glass and made a drink for her. "Sorry there's no ice," he said. She put both hands out to accept the glass from him.

He watched her take a taste, a swallow, nod—and drink another mouthful. "Good," she said.

"I don't know what happened," he began. Then stopped and said, "Of course, I *do* know—what I mean is that I didn't think . . . I mean, I should have—*shouldn't* have. I'm sorry. That was about the

116

last . . . the most . . . oh, I don't know—*pathetic* . . ."

"Don't sweat it," she said solemnly. "You made me feel . . . um, good, real good. What's done is done. And it wasn't all your fault, now was it?" She took another sip. "So how about we think of something else to do instead?"

Phi tried to think. Discuss philosophy some more? Tell jokes? Turn on TV?

"I've got a good idea," she said.

"What's that?" he asked, still ashamed, a bit defensive. He sank down in the maple armchair, dropping his discarded shirt and outer shorts onto the floor.

"Let's play sort of twenty questions, anything we want to ask," she said, "a few each at a time. But here's the rules: the other person swears to answer truthfully. And the person asking swears they'll never tell the answers to another living soul."

Philo'd never liked these kinds of games. They always struck him as not only childish/girlish but also potentially discomforting. When forced to play them, he would keep his options open—i.e., lie. Except right now he didn't want to; he was tired, and he owed her something. On top of that, there were some things about her that he'd kind of like to know, himself. He knew *she* wouldn't lie.

"Okay," he said. And, "You ask first." He'd let her set the tone.

"All right," she said. "Let's see. How about . . . Does Philo Fortune have a special girl back home?" He began to roll his eyes around; he couldn't help himself, it was a reflex, this was just so . . . so *typical.* "I'm not looking for a name or a description," she tacked on.

Philo sighed. Then thought: Come on, you said you would, and where's the harm?

"No, not really," he conceded. "Not if you mean someone I'm in love with, or go steady with, or anything like that. Of course," he added hastily, "there *are* some girls I like and see a lot." Not to give the wrong idea.

She nodded, sipped again, and said, "Well, have you *ever* had a really special girlfriend? You know, someone you were reallyreally tight with, someone absolutely special?"

Philo took a swallow of his drink and smiled. "Back in fourth—or maybe it was fifth grade, I'm not sure—I fell in love with this one girl, Amelia. But I'm pretty sure she never knew it, even though I stayed In love with her for—oh, two years, I guess." Then he smiled at that. "I'd imagine she was queen of Spain and I was Christopher Columbus—except in real life I was much too shy to speak to her."

He'd never mentioned his Age of Discovery period to a girl before—not counting his mother, of course—and he hadn't thought about Amelia (whose folks had moved out of town the fall he started junior high) for centuries. He started fooling with the top of the vodka bottle, near him on the table.

"Could I have a little more of that?" Thea held her glass out; it was empty.

"Does that count as a question?" Philo said, but kiddingly, relaxed. And, "Sure, why not? I'll have some more myself. We don't have to have a designated driver." He poured for both of them, not really sure if he was making "normal" drinks, like in a bar, or not. Not caring, either.

"So," said Thea, with a good grip on her glass again. "Just out of curiosity, not at all important. *Have* you ever done it with a girl?" And when he only looked at her, looked blank and didn't speak she added, "*You* know, had *intercourse*."

"No." He said it frankly, manfully, feeling wholly what-the-hell. Why not tell the truth? Even if it didn't make him look . . . oh, cool and macho. As long as he'd been dating, he had lied (a lot) to girls, although he hadn't thought of it as lying. He'd called it kidding around. Well, maybe it was time to cut that out, to level with a girl for once. He thought that might feel kind of nice. And besides, he'd never been sure those earlier girls had respected him a whole lot, even the ones who'd kidded him right back and seemed impressed by his ambition, and his future plans. Thea, on the other hand, hadn't seemed at all impressed by those things. It was pretty clear she'd prefer to hang out with . . . more the kind of guy his *mother* wanted him to be.

"No, not really," he went on. "I've had what happened here, like, happen with a girl, on purpose. You know—when the two of you are sort of fooling around. But that was pretty much instead of having intercourse—*you* know."

And Thea'd only nodded, looking serious and thoughtful—*understanding*, Philo would have said. He tried to guess—imagine—what she'd ask him next. Turned out he missed it by a mile.

"What's your family consist of?" was the question. "You got any brothers, any sisters? Are your parents like, together, or divorced?"

Philo said no, his folks were not divorced. He said he thought they probably were pretty much like lots of people's parents, except for maybe being smarter, or at least more highly educated, than a lot of others are.

And then he settled back in his chair and told her lots about his mother and his father, and even some about his younger sister, Marietta. Going just by what he said, a listener (he realized) would think he was a really lucky guy (except financially, of course), the son of people who were pretty cool and really cared about him. But (he also thought) those *were* the facts, no doubt about it. And, in further fact, his background sort of made him kind of special, that he sprang from loins like theirs.

Before he'd even noticed he was doing it, he'd gone beyond the boundaries of her question and told her many other things, as well—about his town, and school, and Eddie Skiles, "the Scoper." And then he got to talking about this trip that he was on, and why he'd started out on it, originally—the questions that he'd hoped to get the answers to, that kind of stuff. But before he knew it, he found himself saying—and even actually believing—that being on his own the way he was, meeting new people, was giving him some new perspectives, maybe even insights into . . . life, and himself, and his priorities. And how *that* was becoming the best part about the trip—"maybe especially the 'new people' part." Before he finished up, he'd told her—wanted to tell her—where he thought he'd (he might have actually said *"they'd"*) go next, from there, and where after that, and after that. It was fun, he found, to sit there swigging at a drink and being *real,* confiding in this very pretty girl. Sharing lots of stuff with her.

When Philo finally did come to, he stopped the mono-
logue and quickly tried to change the subject.

"But, hey," he said. "Too much of me, already. Time
to pitch some questions your way, right?"

Thea looked at him and licked her lips as if she
were about to speak. But then she seemed to change
her mind; she shrugged and made a little gesture with
one hand, a "go ahead." She'd drunk two drinks in
not a lot of time, and now, he thought, she looked
significantly smashed. Her covers had slipped down
so that he now could see the tops of both her breasts.
She still had both hands wrapped around her empty
glass, perhaps afraid that someone—he—might try to
take it from her.

He had no such plans. He was floating, feeling great,
his earlier . . . mistake put well behind him. He
wanted to know more about her, all about her, really.
Between the two of them, they'd build (to use his
mother's metaphor) a fine, familiar structure, get it
nicely done before they tried to put the spire on again.
It wasn't any stretch to say he loved her, and he

thought perhaps she understood him better, now. Plus, lying there like that, she sure looked cute.

"So, how about yourself," he said lightheartedly. "You got a boyfriend waitin' by the gate, back home? Singin' love songs underneath your window? Strummin' on his old banjo?" He might have been a little buzzed himself. He was pretty sure she didn't have a boyfriend. Face it, *she'd* suggested all of this.

"No," she said. "I . . . *absolutely no.*"

"Aha!" said Phi. "But you did have one, correct? The two of you broke up—had, like, a knock-down-drag-out fight—and then you packed your case, picked up your sign, and hit the road." He smiled—a wide, all-knowing one. "Howzat for a guess? On target? Pretty warm?"

"No," she said. "You're colder than Alaska, than Antarctica. If you got much colder . . . well, your spit would freeze."

"Huh," said Philo. "I'm surprised. But never mind. Hup-two, question three, the biggie. And remember that we swore to tell the truth. No need to be embarrassed, either, not with Cap'n Philo; he's broadminded as they come. So—ready with the drumroll? Question three: Have you, the princess *Theodora,* ever done it?"

And he lolled back in his chair, another grin in place.

She might have smiled; her lips moved, anyway. It *could* have been "Broad-minded?" that he lip-read, that she didn't say. And when she started speaking, it was very softly, yes, so softly that at first he thought she *was* embarrassed, which would have been a first for her, in his experience.

"Have I ever done it?" Thea said. She didn't look at him but at the ceiling and the farthest corner of the room. "Have I ever *done* it? Hmm, lessee. What shall I answer, truthfully? Maybe better to rephrase the question, Cap'n. Put it this way, right? Has she, the princess Theodora"—she slurred the title so it sounded more like "prishess"—"ever had it done *to* her, by anyone? Like, jus' for an example, by her mother's first-string boyfriend, Jeff? Big bopper Jeff, all right? And after that by Jeffie's li'l bopper brother, Davey, maybe?"

Her voice had gotten somewhat louder and much blurrier. Philo thought, She's drunk—or maybe *crazy*. What was she laying on him? That her mother's boyfriend had *attacked* her? And his *brother*, too? Had she been reading motorcycle-gang memoirs, or what? He'd heard some pretty gross tales—rumors, really—at his school. There was, supposedly, a family that lived down at the trailer park, but hey, *this* stuff? He saw the dog's head had come up, up high, and she was looking up at Thea sharply—looking worried (even), Philo thought.

"Now, even though you didn' ask," Thea now was saying, "you may very well be wondering about where Prishess Theodora's *mother* was, if and/or when this kinda shit began." She put one hand above her eyebrows as she peered up at the ceiling, all around the room. "Good question, that. Where *was* her royal majesty? Uh-oh! Why, *there* she is, squirmin' on the other bed with tricky-dicky-Davey and his magic cobra, boys and girls!" She nodded then, just staring at one spot. "Hey, you best believe it. There they are, all four of them, all right!" She dropped her hand, and now her eyes were squeezed shut tight, as if she was in pain.

"Have I ever done it?" she asked softly. "Hey, I did not only it, but this and that, and then the other thing." Her voice got hoarse and strained. "Jeff said

123

he'd kill me if I didn't, right? But you know what? I didn't *ever* love it, like he said I would. I hated it. I never asked for it, I always—"

For some reason, right at that point there, her eyes snapped open, and she looked at Philo squarely. Really stared at him.

Later on, he tried to guess—to remember—what he must have looked like at that moment. There were lots of possibilities. *Horrified* was likely, maybe even *scared.* Conceivably—he hated thinking this—*disgusted.*

"What?" she snarled. Her eyes were wide and shiny. "What's wrong with *you*?" He thought she looked at him as if he'd just slid out from under slime. "You 'fraid you've caught some bad disease from touching me? Or, no—you're thinking that I must have made this up, that I'm some kind of mental, right?" She was breathing harder, and her face seemed twisted, different. "Is that what's bugging you, sweet, sheltered little baby, Philo Forshun? That you've been hangin' out with somebody *insane*?"

"Hell, no," he said defensively. "You couldn't be more wrong." He let out a nervous laugh. He wasn't sure that he knew how to cope with this. "So take it easy; I'm just—"

"Take it . . . *what*?" she yelped, and threw her glass at him, sitting up in bed to do so. It whizzed by his left ear and thunked into the rug, behind him. He jumped up, not feeling any part of carefree anymore. He'd never had a girl do anything like that to him before.

"You *bum*," she shrieked at him. "I bet that's all you ever think about, is how you're gonna do that: take it easy, take it *from* somebody, easy. Take everything off everyone, real easy. Go ahead, admit it. You took all this real easy, didn't you?" She cupped her breasts for just a second; Philo bent and snatched his shirt and

124

shorts off the floor. "All they cost you was some acting and some easy little lies, you rotten bastard. Well, to *hell* with you!"

She started getting out of bed. "Go on," she yelled. "You've got your clothes; you want to go? Get out of here!" She was on her feet and picking up the vodka bottle. She held it by the neck and stood there frozen for a moment, swaying slightly, looking fuzzy and uncertain. The dog had also gotten up and now was looking back and forth between her mistress and the boy.

Philo, with his shorts and shirt clutched tightly to his chest, had started backing toward the door. This, he thought, is like a story or a nightmare, something unbelievable. Way, way beyond the boundaries of his comfort zone or even his imaginings. He figured that he could subdue the girl—grapple with her, get her down, disarm her by brute force—but that wasn't on his want-to list at all. What he wanted was the thing she'd said: to get the hell away from there, and her, as far away, and as fast as he could go. Her suggesting it was like a little bonus, full permission, Mother said I could.

He tucked the clothes under one arm, so he'd have both hands free for suitcase, backpack, and the door.

"Look," he said, on automatic pilot now. "How about I go and get us both some coffee and a sandwich, maybe . . ." He reached behind him, blindly, for the doorknob.

That set her off again. She slammed the bottom of the pint against the writing table's edge. It broke, but not the way that bottles do in movies. This one came apart up by the neck, so she was left with just a little stub of slivered glass, way up near her hand. She looked at it, and him, again.

"You know something?" she said, and now her voice was just a whisper, clogged. "I *hate* you and your

125

damn dumb car, and what you eat and drink and think an' . . . everything." And she started whooping up great sobs. "You wouldn' know . . . what virtue was . . . if it jumped up . . . and bit you on the ass . . . An' I just *hate* you . . . Philo Forshun . . . you don' love me . . . any more than . . . anyone."

At least she's not coming toward me, Philo thought. For the moment, she was simply standing there, crying, breathing hard, looking in a way ridiculous, naked with that little—*dangerous* little—weapon in her hand.

He had no more to say. He popped the room door open and bent to lift the suitcase and the backpack. But as he straightened up, she stumbled toward him, leading with that tiny dagger.

It hit and tore, but mostly in the jumbled roll of clothing that he'd stuck between his chest and arm. He felt a kind of bee sting on his arm, but nothing terrible; her little weapon tumbled to the floor.

In the next breath he was out of there, the door kicked shut behind him (he heard an "Oh my god . . ." before it slammed), and running for the car. Beside the Squareback, seeing that the door to Unit 5 was staying shut, he paused to slip his shirt and torn shorts on, the ones that had—thank God!—the car keys in their pocket, still. While doing that, he noticed he was cut, there on the biceps, not that badly. Once in the car, he got a tissue out, blotted up the blood, and threw it out the window.

He'd left his running shoes behind. But, hell, he'd driven barefoot lots of times. He no longer felt the least bit drunk—just thankful for being out of there, relieved.

For the first few minutes, Philo drove the Squareback leaning forward, with the steering wheel almost against his chest. He looked a little like a jockey, urging on his mount, or like a wheelman fleeing from a bank job and expecting bullets from behind. Only when his shoulder muscles started cramping did he notice the position he was in, lean back against the seat, and make himself breathe normally again. He glanced down at his cut; it wasn't even bleeding anymore.

She's nuts; she's really nuts! was most of what he thought the first two miles, along with Was she really trying to kill me?

Suppose, he mused after a while, suppose she'd had a gun, instead. Would she have shot me? She'd absolutely said she hated him, all right. Imagine: someone *hating* him and trying to *kill* him. Someone who was a *girl.* A girl might try to slap him on the wrist, perhaps, not hard—but kill him? They always knew he'd stop, if that was what they wanted. This scenario was altogether different—like, impossible.

And totally unfair, he thought. He hadn't been that bad. There wasn't any reason she should hate him. True, he hadn't played a starring role in *Motel Madness* (no one under 17 admitted). But, as she herself conceded, that wasn't all his fault.

No, she—this Theodora girl—was totally irrational. He should have guessed that when he heard her weirdo name. And again after she told him all that virtue-is-the-only-good crap. Hey—she was some advertisement for Cynicism, wasn't she? How about *her* deeds? She was supposedly typifying virtue, right? What would that Diogenes—the guy—have said if he had seen her going after someone with a broken vodka bottle?

Of course it *was* true that the vodka was his fault; he admitted that, around mile ten. He had bought the vodka and had even poured her drinks. And she had gotten drunk. And that had been the trouble, *a* big trouble. When she'd gotten drunk, she'd gone a little crazy. If she hadn't gotten drunk, she probably wouldn't have started hating him that way—just because he hadn't kept a stupid look from showing on his face.

But he hadn't tried to *get her* drunk. He'd bought the vodka for himself, to help himself relax and get a little carefree. He hadn't planned for her to drink it; she had *asked* to. He knew from his own experience at parties, and seeing other kids get really smashed, that there was no predicting what a drunken kid might say or do. Surely she knew that as well as he did. And you'd also think she'd know how she could handle alcohol. She wasn't any baby; she had been around a lot. A whole lot more than she—or anyone—would want to be around, he guessed.

That got him to reviewing all she'd said. She'd gotten very drunk and then she started talking. If the stuff she'd said was true, she really was a major hurter—as well as (maybe) crazy. She'd been holding in this awful secret (it could have been a good long while), and the vodka'd made her uninhibited enough to blurt it out to him. To somebody—he squirmed as he remembered this—who'd told her that he *loved* her.

Of course he *didn't* love her (he now told himself) and never had. It had just been something that he'd said, a thing that one specific moment seemed to call for. In all honesty, he might have *thought* it at the time, under the influence of . . . her. How she'd come on to him, her looks and all. But he hadn't *loved* her, couldn't have. You didn't love the sort of person who was capable of trying to *kill* you—did you?

He was, it now occurred to him, extremely lucky he had learned . . . well, all the stuff he had. Before they spent a lot more time together. If all that hadn't happened, and they'd kept on being sidekicks on this trip, well, naturally, a greater friendship would have probably sprung up between the two of them. It was even possible they'd have gotten to be lovers in a much more normal way, after having gone through all the other, lower levels in the wondrous world of make out. Like what his *mother'd* talked about! One thing was for sure: he'd never know that now.

He guessed she was what he'd heard guys call damaged goods. He'd never gone for that expression, personally. And he wouldn't really say that it applied to Thea, even now. She might be plenty—or a little—crazy, but that was where it stopped and started. He *was* glad that he'd escaped from an . . . entanglement with her. But until she'd gotten drunk and started thinking that she hated him (and tried to *kill* him, don't forget), she had seemed no different than a lot of girls, except maybe better-looking, overall. She hadn't felt, to him, like damaged goods at all.

About mile twenty-five, Philo realized he was ravenous, perhaps the hungriest he'd ever been. But, providentially, a little ways ahead, there were the friendly lights of a substantial Mini-Mart and Deli. Instant food, he thought; come on. The car had barely stopped when he was out of it and through the market's door.

The smell inside came through his nostrils; twin streams of deliciousness went racing up his nose. One went to his brain (it seemed) where it became the words *roast chicken!* The other headed south, down to his stomach, which said, "Gimme!"

Five minutes later, he was sitting in the car again, tearing at a hot, whole, greasy little fryer, painted reddish-brown by burned-on spicy sauce. On the seat beside him was a tub that held potato salad and a plastic fork. Between his thighs was jammed a giant Pepsi— liter size. Waiting on the floor, a bag of Pecan Sandies. Dinner! A passerby would probably have noticed something else: for the first two minutes there, Philo grunted as he ate.

Once the knife-edge of his hunger had been dulled, his eating slowed—and quieted as well. He started using the napkins that the deli guy had given him. He began to feel a lot more like himself, and so he started making plans.

He decided, first, that he would find another motel room, another cheap one. After all he'd been through, he thought he ought to get a good night's sleep, that he deserved one. Also, once he found a place to stay, he figured he'd find a phone and give his mom a call. He'd promised, after all, and this'd be his third night on the road. He wouldn't want her—them—to worry.

Beyond that, he was looking forward to doing just

what he'd said he'd planned to do, back in the motel: head on out of this area, get down into another part of the world, where maybe he could get some new perspectives on . . . stuff. He remembered telling *her* that had already happened, and that the best part of the trip had been the new people that he'd met (meaning her) and what he'd sort of . . . *learned* from them. Well, now he definitely wanted to meet some *other* new people and maybe get back to basics, to that getting-a-bead-on-America business and learning how to be a killer whale. Maybe he was better off sticking to his original . . . personality. He thought he'd give those questions of his another try. They hadn't worked too well in Garston, but that didn't mean there was something wrong with them. It could have been the Garstonites. But on the off chance that the guy in the Cadillac could have been the least bit right, he'd even dress a little better next time, maybe put on his father's jacket, or something. Nice clothes might make him look a little older and more serious.

Then, after that stop, he planned to head up into Eddie country. It might be a kick to see the Scoper at this back-to-the-boonies place, with his thin veneer of manners stripped away, a wild man in the wilds!

Thinking of Eddie brought Thea back to his mind. Or not so much *Thea* as Thea's place in myth and legend, as a player in the screenplay of *The Life of Philo Fortune* (as told by Fortune, P.). Suppose he *did* find Eddie—or suppose he didn't, that he didn't see him until Labor Day, back home. Would he tell him any version of the Thea story—real, condensed, or reshaped to his advantage? He knew it would make old Eddie's eyes bug out at lots of different points along the way.

But he wasn't sure, at this point, he was going to . . . share the tale. Some stories weren't for general consumption—for Eddie-fication, you could say—nor should every detail of his life be made available to *anyone.* Tanya, now, he'd surely talk about. Tanya was the sort of pearl he'd gladly throw in front of Eddie: her corporeal exposures in the front seat of his car. Eddie would go wild, imagining the girl accountant. "Audit *this,* baby," he might shout. "Lemme see that lovely bottom line!"

The Safe Harbor Motor Court looked perfect for his cheapskate purposes, Phi thought. Judging by its signs, or lack thereof, the place was not approved by anyone—not AAA, nor ALA, nor ASCAP. Like Jomar's it was small, about a dozen units, and not new; it clearly wasn't part of any chain. It did have customers, however—just a few. Basic, American-made sedans were parked outside almost half the units, and apparently their drivers had already gone to bed; Phi saw no lights in windows, other than those in the office. The time was a quarter after ten.

Before he went inside, he slipped a cotton sweater on and wriggled into jeans; peering in the rearview mirror, he also brushed his hair. He could have put on moccasins, but figured being barefoot wouldn't matter.

There was no one in the office when he entered it, but he heard some talking coming through a curtained door behind the counter—talking he soon recognized as coming from a radio or television set. The speaker seemed to have a major bitch about the way a lot of folks were carrying on, these days.

A silver bell was sitting on the countertop, and Phi hit it, open handed, hard. Nothing happened. He stood there, shifting his weight and wondering about an encore, when suddenly a man popped through the curtain. It was as if he'd been standing right behind it all the time. The guy was small and bald, round-shouldered with a pointed chin and rimless specs, a cardigan. He shot a boyward glance that could have passed (the boy opined) for genuine dislike.

"Good evening," Philo said to him. "You got a room for me tonight?"

The man then looked him over slowly, head to toe—bare toe. He looked as if he'd tasted something rotten.

"We'd just as soon not rent to kids," he said. But then, surprisingly, "There's just the one of you?" He did ask that suspiciously, however, as if he had a notion barefoot people always came in twos or threes.

"Yep," said Phi. "Just me. I'm pretty sure I don't know anyone for fifty miles around." And he laughed to show that was a little joke he'd made.

"So, you'd be wanting just one night?" the fellow asked. And, when Philo nodded, "Checkout here's at 10 A.M., with no exceptions. And we don't allow no smoking in the units."

"Fine with me," said Phi. "I never started cigarettes." He felt he should say more. "Or snuff or Red Man, either."

"You sure you don't have any animals with you?" the man inquired. He pointed to the sign behind him, where it said No Pets.

"Nope," said Philo. "Like I said, there's only me."

"There's no TV in any of the units," said the man. "And that pool you might have seen out back—it ain't been filled for years."

"No problem," Phi assured him. "I'll be going out to make a phone call, but after that I'm heading straight to bed." Then, inspired, he tacked on, "I promised that I'd call my mom tonight."

For just an eye blink there, the motel owner might have looked . . . oh, mildly pleased. In any case, he

133

sighed and said, "All right. The room is twenty-five, that's tax included, and you pay me now. Leave the key right in the door, tomorra morning." He put a card in front of Philo. "You can gimme your John Henry, here."

Phi pulled his money out and paid, and then wrote, Edward Skiles, 69 Cuttaloosa Way, Libidinous, PA, in his nearly illegible script. The fellow glanced at it and nodded, put the money in his trouser pocket and produced the key to Unit 3.

"Number Three," he said. "And don't forget, no smoking." He turned and went back through the curtain. As he did, Phi heard him say to someone on the other side: "I put a snotnose kid in Number Three for twenty-five. So how about you get your fat ass off the chair and turn the outside light out?"

"Yeah, I know it's late," Phi said. He'd kept the phone booth door open; it smelled, inside, peculiarly of cat. "But I only just now found a place to spend the night— this dumpy little motor court. I didn't want you worrying. You weren't sleeping, were you? . . . You *did?* Hey, Mom, you must be psychic!

"No, way past there. I think I saw a sign that said The Town of Bryce. Hi, Dad—you down there in the kitchen? . . . Yeah, I was telling Mom: I've taken a motel room. The last two nights I stayed out in the boonies, off a little country road. . . . No, not in any *farmhouse,* in the *woods.*

"Maybe fifty-fifty. Some of them are interesting, and some are creeps. 'The people is a beast,' right, Dad? . . . Yeah, I've had some ideas. . . . No, nothing real specific, yet. I'm finding out some things I *wouldn't* want to be, I'll tell you that. . . . Oh, an airline pilot, for example. I think a lot of jerks go into that.

"No, not so far I haven't been. . . . No, if I get

134

bored or anything, I just pick up a hitchhiker. I've been *very* careful, Mom. And I've only picked up two, so far." He laughed. "Yes, both of them—hey, how'd you ever guess? One was a Riddle student, and I dropped her off there at the college. . . . Okay—the other might have been a runaway, I thought. She had this big *dog* with her. No, not my type at all; you got that right.

"It wasn't all that bad, as a matter of fact. What I did was move everything up front, and spread the pad in back. It was pouring when I woke up, yesterday; d'you get lots of rain, yourselves? . . . The food you packed is *perfect,* Mom. I've been eating it for break-fast, lunch, and dinner—right up until tonight. . . . Oh, a deli chicken—barbecued—and some potato salad.

"I think the next two days I'm gonna drive, drive, drive—yeah, it's been running great. . . . I thought I'd run a check on Southern hospitality. . . . No, no—just like before, meet people on the street, or in a lun-cheonette, or park, or something—ask them different questions. . . . That's right, it's an education in itself, just hearing what they say.

"After *that* maybe I will. Who knows if anyone'll even know where Eddie *is*—I mean they do a lot of backpacking, like I told you. But I'd like to see the setup, anyway. What kind of prison Daddy Skiles has dumped his dear boy in. Otherwise, he'll lie to me, if I know Eddie—and I do.

"Pretty good. I haven't had to spend much, so far. The S-back's great on gas, as you well know, and what else is there? As long as Mom's food holds out. . . . Oh—one stupid thing I did, before I forget to tell you: I left my running shoes back at this place where I was camping out. It's so embarrassing; I'd gotten them completely soaked and took them off before I got

135

back in the car to eat and put dry stuff on—and later on I just drove off and left them there. . . . Yeah, you're right; they had some miles on them, but still. . . . Yeah, I'll pick up a pair of cheapos, probably tomorrow.

"Overall? So far? Oh, a good B plus—A minus. I *miss* you guys and everything, but it's gotta be a valuable experience, being on my own and all, having to make all my own decisions. Yeah, sure, I will. . . . You know me—I look before I leap. . . . So—give the kid a pinch for me, okay? . . . No, in the *morning*, Dad, when she wakes up. . . . Yeah, love you, too. . . . You bet; I'll call real soon. G'bye."

There were two single beds, saggy in the middle, and a Bible on the bedside table in between them. In the bathroom there were just two sets of towels and washcloths and no water glasses; the bathroom door was mirror-free.

Phi undressed quickly, checked his cut again, decided it was just a scratch, brushed his teeth and got right into bed. He was really, really tired; it had been some kind of memorable day. To think: he'd almost done it there, with Thea, come a whole lot closer than he ever had before. He looked forward to the day he'd be able to say yes, a truthful yes, to the question Thea'd asked him, the Big Question. He guessed that girls—in college, say—were asking it, some form of it, a lot, these days, with AIDS around, and everything. And guys, too. The weird thing was—the *re*tard thing, perhaps—he'd never asked a girl, before today.

And, suddenly, a most unwelcome thought came to his mind. Was it remotely possible she'd set the whole thing up, to sort of *make* him ask the stuff he did, so she could tell him what had happened to her earlier, back home? Could her getting him to go to a motel with her have been a cry for help (he'd once heard a shrink on *Oprah* use the term)? A cry that he had not been strong enough, or cool enough, or *good* enough to handle?

Nah, he told himself. Impossible. She wouldn't turn to him for help, someone she'd called anti-twin, her opposite. She didn't like him, even know him, all that well. No way . . . not her . . . she was a nutcase, much more likely . . . pure forget-about material. That kind of stuff was not enjoyable to think about. Nor was the recollection of the last he'd seen of her, all naked, stumbling in his direction, staggering . . .

The next morning, to Philo's amazement and horror, the Squareback wouldn't start. Amazement, because it always *had* started; horror, in that he knew a big fat zilch concerning what to do about it.

His dad had taught him all the repair tricks he knew, in half of a Sunday morning: how to use a lug wrench, jack a car up safely, take a tire off and put one on, and finally get your auto lowered back to earth again. But that was it. What went on under the hood—or in this case, the floormat, in back—was pretty much a mystery to both male members of the Fortune family. For different reasons, neither one was interested.

Of course that didn't mean they wouldn't peer and shake their heads and make some clucking noises with their tongues at auto engines. And, to be fair, they knew the *names* of certain automotive parts. They just didn't understand how any of them worked.

So, Philo did exactly what his father would have done, had he been in this fix. He opened up the back of the Squareback, shoved all the luggage forward (there was Thea's sign!), folded back the floormat, and opened up the trapdoor that concealed the pancake engine. Like his father, he, too, harbored the vague hope that there'd be something so obviously wrong in there that (even) he could notice it and, reaching down, slip silly old Tab A back into virtuous Slot B, where it belonged. Which, of course, would mean that Car VW would start right up.

Such was not the case, of course, and Phi just stood there, bent way over, hands on knees, staring at the Squareback engine's marvelous complexity and wondering how someone had ever thought of it.

"Uh-oh—trouble?" said a cheerful voice from right behind him.

Philo, startled, spun around. The man was sandy haired and round faced, of ample girth, and beaming. The clothes he had on—a sleeveless white undershirt, chocolate brown Bermuda shorts, black street shoes, and white athletic socks—suggested to the boy that he was *(a)* a guy of no importance whatsoever, and *(b)* on vacation. His legs and upper arms were pinkish-bluish white.

"Yeah," said Philo ruefully, not turning on much charm. "Darn thing won't start."

"I love these little sweethearts," said the man. "I had three different ones before I let the missus talk me into something bigger." He jerked his head in the direction of the three cars parked to Philo's right. The nearest one, Phi saw, had a woman and two children in it; all three heads were turned in their direction.

"This one here's my mother's car," said Phi, just making conversation, "so I don't really know too much about it." He shrugged. "I hope the manager can tell me who to call." He hoped he wouldn't have to call his mother.

"Old Luke the sourpuss?" But the guy's big smile belied the words. "I'm sure he could and would, God

139

bless his prickly hide. But before you do—go in and ask, I mean—suppose you try to turn it over for me once. It *could* be somethin' I could help you with, real simple. Just let me get a couple things, okay?"

Phi almost didn't get it. The trouble with his car . . . it surely wasn't *this* guy's problem. But what the heck, he thought. So he nodded, muttered "Sure," and watched the man bounce over to the car with all the people in it, say something to them smilingly, and get smiles back from them, along with nods worked into sentences. The guy then opened up his trunk and fished a small red toolbox out.

"Won't leave home without the Good Book or the toolbox," he told Philo, coming back. "Hands to work and hearts to God." He rubbed his hands together. "So, now let's see." He took out a rubber-handled screwdriver. "Suppose you just hop in and turn the key, my friend."

Phi did as he was told. And, as expected, nothing happened.

"Hold it," called the man, bent over in the back. "Okay, now try it."

This time—wow!—a miracle occurred. The engine started instantly, making its familiar putt-putt-putter.

". . . what I thought," the guy was saying. "You can shut it off. Once in a blue moon, the little *framissonic* valve gets stuck and all you gotta do is tweak the *gasserator* under there a little and she frees right up." (That's sort of what his diagnosis sounded like to Philo, anyway.) "Won't happen in another hundred thousand miles, I'll bet."

"Golly!" Phi exclaimed. "That's wonderful! Amazing! I can't believe you fixed it—just like that." Knowing what came next—believing in it, even—he reached into his pocket. "Here. What do I owe you?"

"Hey, my pleasure," said the man. "I couldn't take your money, son. We were neighbors, just last night now, weren't we?" He waved toward their units.

"I guess we were," said Phi. "But still. That was so *great* of you." He stuck out his hand without thinking, still so relieved, that he was almost hyperventilating. "I'm Philo Fortune, high school student on a trip. I just wish that there was some way I could pay you back."

The round-faced man had a warm, firm grip. "Jack Frederick," he informed the boy. "Pastor-slash-mechanic with the wife and kids on our vacation. And hey, the way that you can do us *both* a favor is for you to do the same: give someone else a hand one day."

"Uh — *right*," said Philo. "Sure." Thinking: a couple of bucks would have made for a much . . . neater transaction.

"I'll surely try to do that, Mr. Frederick," he went on. Thinking, I said "try."

"All right, then, Philo," said the man. "You have yourself a nice safe journey, now. God bless."

"Absolutely," Philo said, saluting him and moving toward the Squareback's door. "You, too."

He really *was* indebted to this modern Friar Tuck, this jolly little . . . *tweakmaster.*

After breakfasting on supermarket doughnuts with a quart of milk (and a complimentary coffee, in the aisles), Philo hit the interstate. It'd take him pretty near the next place that he planned to visit.

This time, thanks to his earlier experience, he hardly ever left the right-hand lane of the big road; he buzzed along contentedly at close to sixty, with the Squareback's not-so-hotsy radio providing all the company he needed. Hitchhiking was illegal on the interstate; yeah, damn straight. By the time he got so

141

hungry that he had to stop, he'd put almost two hundred miles behind him.

That was good, but it also raised a question. If he kept on interstating all that day and part of the next (but could he stand to do that?), he'd reach the exit nearest to his next stopping place well before sundown, he realized. That was the town called Acheron, county seat of Corbett County. Early on, when he had just begun to plan the trip, he decided that he had to check out Acheron, see what-all was shakin' there. He'd grinned the moment he saw it on the map. He was sure there were important truths to be revealed in such a town, no matter that it was slightly off the beaten track, not in a wealthy Northeast state. Anytime he talked about his trip to anyone, he always mentioned he was going to go to Acheron. Most people didn't get it, only shrugged.

As he started heading out of the rest area where he'd eaten his lunch, he was still a little undecided on the question of the interstate. As he turned it over in his mind, though, he saw—amazingly!—another Squareback pulling in, just as he was pulling out. And more than that, its driver honked at him and stuck a bare arm out the window, giving him a huge and friendly wave. The person had short hair and wore a pair of racy runner's shades.

He couldn't help but take that as a sign. This was a road that catered to his kind of car, his kind of player. It was a user-friendly road, for him. He swung back on the highway, whistling, his mind made up.

So, that afternoon, he made good time again. At first it was a little boring, passing by the edges of some unattractive cities and through long stretches of . . . oh, preindustrial America: hills with trees on them, and fields. The possibilities for more controlled development seemed almost endless.

But then his mind slid back to Thea and stayed there for a while.

She'd probably had quite a hangover this morning, he supposed. Obviously, she hadn't been too used to booze; either that or she was one of those people who get real sauced real fast. (He wondered if she remembered every little thing that happened in those last fifteen minutes in the room—how he'd reacted to her awful story, the expression on his face that made her go bananas, made her hate him.)

Anyway, she'd probably waked up feeling as if she had a couple of construction crews inside her head, busy roofing an entire housing project. And while that hammering was going on, she probably got back to hating Philo Fortune.

She'd think that she had reason to, all right; he couldn't help but count the ways. One: for being such a jerk and taking all those peeks at Tanya. Two: for being such a jerk in bed (even if that wasn't all his fault). Three: for having bought that vodka in the first place. Four: for being so uncool about her awful history. And finally, five: for bugging out of not just Jomar's but the area (and shortly after that, the state), leaving her in that motel perhaps without a nickel to her name and one big dog (in addition to herself) to feed. He was awfully, awfully glad his mom would never learn how he'd behaved with Thea.

Or heard the things she'd said about him, just before he left that motel room.

He shifted in his seat and stretched his right leg briefly. He wanted to change the subject in his mind. The last . . . oh, fifteen minutes of that time with Thea (which, face it, were the last fifteen minutes he'd ever spend with her) were nowhere near his finest quarter hour. Even if you took into consideration that he *had* done quite a bit for her *previously*—driving her and her huge hound around, going along with her far-out suggestions—he could not be proud of how he'd handled things. So he'd had a few drinks himself and hadn't been in the best of moods—so (really) what?

But the girl, beyond a doubt, was too messed up for anyone with any sense to get involved with. To be fair, he now was pretty sure she hadn't tried to kill him; that cut had come by accident—a drunken stumble—and was so minor that it almost didn't count. Plus, he *had* heard her call out "Oh my God . . ." (he just remembered) as if she'd been scared stiff she'd really hurt him. It was just too bad he hadn't had a chance to tell his side of . . . everything, before the two of them split up. But things just hadn't worked out that way. It wasn't anybody's fault. What happened, happened. *Shit* happens (Philo thought, and shook his head regretfully), just like the bumper sticker says.

It was weird—and pretty scary—how different this whole Thea thing had been from anything that had happened—ever—with the girls he'd known before. The Lisas and the Ronis, they were *high school girls.* He'd gone on dates with them, and he and they alike had played a bunch of little games with one another. Childish little dating types of games. He might make some move, and they would either counter or allow it. Then it might be their turn to get something out of *him*—a present that they wanted, or to have him take them somewhere.

But this thing with Thea had been different, altogether different—more like an affair, a *love* affair. The stakes had seemed much higher and the issues they had gotten into so much larger, more defining. Neither Roni nor Lisa would have ever walked all night in the rain to get to him—would have cared so much about a promise or, let's face it, *him.* And they sure would never have given him a whole bunch of their money, called him "keeper of the cash," their cash. Or sobbed, for fear they might have hurt him.

And he would never have been so . . . unevasive with the two of them, or so interested in what they thought. It was hard to think of Roni having a philosophy—other than Let's Party!

Finally, there was him saying that he loved her—Thea—and having her accept that and not tell him to shut up.

Maybe—Philo sighed—his luck, his life, *was* changing. This trip had already been so much more . . . *maturing* (he supposed that was the proper word) than he'd ever in the world expected it would be. Now, possibly, the roads and towns ahead of him would be stuffed with girls more beautiful and interesting (and far more sane) than Thea. Just waiting for the chance to have their own good Fortune (and give him other insights into . . . everything).

Excellent as that thought was, he still felt . . . bummed. He was on his way to Acheron, the day was clear, the track was fast, the car was running perfectly again. He should have been in Pink Cloud City.

He peered ahead, hoping that there might be another Squareback, heading south this time, that he could overtake, and honk, and wave at. For the first time since his folks had gotten it, he actually was glad he had a funky little even-ministers-can-fix-it kind of car.

Phi spent that night parked in a giant service area, right beside the interstate. He spread the pad there in the back again and slept inside the Squareback. The pad, or sleeping bag, he couldn't tell which one (it possibly was both) *did* smell of dog and maybe something (someone?) else, a little. Thea hadn't been the sort to use perfume—Lisa loved White Shoulders; he should know, he had to buy her some, one time—but there was still a fragrance that she had; he remembered that.

In the morning, he treated himself to an early breakfast at the counter of the service area's restaurant, surrounded by a bunch of guys that he was pretty sure were truckers. Philo ordered ham and eggs, just like a lot of them were having, and it came with not only a stack of toast but also some other white stuff on the plate that looked like a hot cereal he used to eat, called Cream of Wheat.

"I didn't order that," he told the countergirl as she was laying down his plate, pointing at the runny white.

"You don't want your grits?" she asked, in some surprise. "They free."

Philo blinked a time or two. *Grits?* He'd read the word, but never heard it said before, and hadn't had the slightest idea what they looked like. Wow, he thought, I guess I'm in the South, all right. I'm going to eat some *grits.*

"Well, in that case, fine," he said. "Sure I want 'em, if they're free." He smiled at her. "Real nice of you," he added. "Right neighborly."

Actually, he didn't like the grits much, but he made sure he cleaned his plate, just as all the truckers did.

Driving out of the area, he passed a line of big tractor-trailers, parked but ready to go, some with their engines already idling. Out of the corner of his eye, he saw there was a dog, alone, in one of them, a big dog sitting by the driver's seat; it could have been a sibling of that Genie's. Of course he knew it wasn't *her,* but still there was a slight disturbance in the center of his body. The *grits,* no doubt, he told himself, and sped out on the interstate again.

Phi stayed on that interstate as long as it made sense.
When he got off it, in the middle of a white-hot afternoon—a sizzler—he still had ninety miles to go before
he got to Acheron, on Highway 24.

Piece of cake, he told himself, and kept on going.
Driving through the open country, he was constantly
being hit by scented, moving air; he was a whole lot
cooler than he would have been if he had stopped.
From time to time, he *did* stop, though, to buy another ice-cold Coca-Cola. He thought it *did* taste different in the South, as he had heard—richer, stronger,
buzzier.

The miles slipped by quite rapidly. Strip mining had
been big in this part of the state, where the coal was
near the planet's skin, but lately, it appeared, no one
was working in those mines. There were a lot of corn-
fields planted, though, as well as other crops that Phi
could not identify, and there was ample wooded land
as well. This is the rural South all right, he thought, as
he drove by dilapidated houses, some of them with
children sitting in their open doorways, looking too

worn out to even wave. Or maybe just too hot. All the kids were barefoot; the girls in simple dresses, the boys bare-chested and in pull-on shorts. There were a lot of pickups on the road.

Acheron, as county seat, was clearly quite the town. Long before he got to it, he started seeing signs that bragged on all the things that lay ahead. There were motels aplenty, even one hotel, the Lyman Corbett. There were also auto agencies and farm supplies and barbecue available, as well as outlet centers, ice-cream stands, and guns and ammunition. The Acheron Red Devils football team would soon attempt to win its third straight Class B title.

He was still some fifteen miles from town when he came upon "Mizzus" Beaufort Cartwright. When he first caught sight of her, he didn't know that it was she, of course. What he saw was a respectable-looking older lady, standing by a car. She was blotting at her face with . . . not a tissue (it turned out), but a linen handkerchief with her initials on it and staring at the left rear tire of her Escort, which was flat. Phi thought her body language said that she was horrified. And, of course, completely helpless.

As he sped on by the woman and the car, she happened to look up. Then he was struck by something else. She seemed amazed to see him.

He started braking just a little after that. He really couldn't *not.* In hardly any time at all, he'd figured out the following: (1) She'd been amazed not at the sight of him so much as at his not stopping to help her; (2) Jack Frederick, his own benefactor, had asked that he help someone else, sometime, and doing so would serve to wipe his conscience clean—or better, put his books in balance; and (3) his dad owned an Escort, meaning this was just the kind of car that he had practiced on, the kind of car whose tires he was *good* at changing.

And, finally, this: a stop might be *worthwhile.*

He made a U-turn, drove back past her once again, made another U, and brought the Squareback to a stop behind the Escort, on the shoulder of the road.

" 'Afternoon," he told the woman, getting out. "Looks like you could use a little help."

"You're from out of state," she said, nodding at his license plate. "A Yankee boy."

"I guess I am," said Philo. He could feel his accent softening, however, imitating hers. He'd always fancied Southern-sounding talk.

"You went on by me, once," she said. "Not to my surprise." He knew that she was lying.

"I'm afraid my mind was wandering," the boy replied. "It took a while before it registered—that you were stuck here, with a flat. But when it did, I turned around and came right back."

She nodded, taking all that in, accepting it, Phi thought. She even offered him a little smile. "You know how to change a tire on this car?"

"Absolutely, ma'am," he said. "My fa—daddy's—got an Escort, too. This is the car I learned to change a tire on. Now, if I could have the key, I'll get your jack out and the spare." In his mind, he was going through the steps involved in proper tire changing.

"Well, all right," she said. "But you be careful, now." She reached in and got the keys from her ignition, gave them to the boy. "I guess you know which one."

Philo did, and before long he was hard at work, the hubcap off and looking like a soup plate, lying there, while he was loosening the lug nuts. He could feel the sweat break out, not just on his brow but all over.

While he worked, the woman stood a little bit away

from him, as if she hadn't any part in what was going on. But she still talked in his direction.

"It's *much* too hot, today," she started. "This isn't normal for the time of year—you probably was wondering. I can't remember when it's been this warm in August. And generally, we have a breeze. My sister's son, the one they all call Scooter, he *says* he keeps the service records on this car, and he's the one who tells me when I ought to have the tires put on different wheels—whatever they call *that,* some word I can't recall—or even if I ought to get some new. He's son to one of my older sisters, Mizzus R. L. Pickens. *I'm* Mizzus Beaufort Cartwright; Mr. Cartwright passed away in nineteen eighty-five. But anyways, the point is, Scooter Pickens should have known this tire was wore out, or no-account to start with. He works for F. B. Jones Ford-Lincoln-Mercury, so that'd be his *job* to know that kind of thing, it seems to me. Doesn't that sound right to you? What did you say your name was, anyway? Or did you ever say?"

"I don't believe I did," said Phi. He'd just got the tire off, and now he had it standing up between his knees while he examined it. "It's Philo, Philo Fortune. And—oops, hey, lookee here. Seems like you picked up a nail somewhere." He pointed to the one embedded in the tire tread.

"Philo," Mizzus Cartwright repeated. "That is *not* a common name, at least in Corbett County. Yes, I can see the nail, all right. I suppose it wasn't there when Scooter looked last time. You going to stop with us in Acheron—or keep on going through? You don't have kin down here, by any chance?"

"No," said Phi. "Regrettably, I don't. But, yes, I hope to spend, oh, two, three days in Acheron, at least. I understand it's quite a town, the county seat and all. I'm looking forward to . . . well, seeing all the sights, and meeting . . . Acheronians, such as yourself." He had the spare on now and had picked up the hub-cap—now with lug nuts floating in it—and was starting to screw them back on with his fingers, as far as he could make them go.

"That's nice," said Mizzus Cartwright. "We have some lovely homes in Acheron, and as picturesque a courthouse square as you will find in this or any other state. Times being what they are, our downtown business area is not quite what it used to be, right now. But everyone's been saying that it's got to come back, soon. Scooter told me F. B. Jones is moving Lincoln Town Cars off the lot again."

Philo worked the jack and eased the car back to the ground. Then he used the wrench to get the lug nuts supertight. Finally—wham!—he slapped the hubcap back in place.

"There you be," he said, as he picked up the damaged tire and took it to the trunk. "Just don't forget to drop this baby off at your garage and get it fixed."

"Well, you stand still and let me give you something for your trouble, Philo Fortune," Mizzus Cartwright said. "You saved me having to stand out in that hot sun a minute longer than I had to. Although I suspect that *someone* I knew pretty well'd have to come along, sometime."

"No, that's all right, ma'am," Philo said, holding up his hand defensively against the . . . threat of money (ho-ho-ho). "My parents taught me to help out whoever was in need, not with reward in mind but as a matter of propriety and principle." Minus the highfalu-tin language, that actually was true. So up until now he hadn't been a real fast learner.

"*Well,*" she said. "That's nice to know—that there's still young people with what many say are just old-fashioned values." She smiled and cocked her head at him, looking downright flirty. "On behalf of all her citizens, I welcome you to Acheron. You'll be a fine addition to our proud, but struggling, community. Now, having said that much, suppose I ask you this: Where were you thinking you might stay here, Philo?"

"Oh, I don't know," he said. "Probably in *there*." He pointed at his car. "I curl up in the back, most nights. That's about the only way to stay within my budget."

"In the back of *that,* you plan to sleep?" said Mizzus Cartwright. "No. I won't stand for that; you'll have to stop with me. I've got the spare room all made up, already. It won't be any trouble, none at all. You can come and go the same as you'd do in a big hotel. You'll not be sleeping in any old car in Acheron. Not after all you've done for Mizzus Beaufort Cartwright."

Phi resisted feebly and not for long. And so, within five minutes he had written down her address on his clipboard, along with how to get there. He said he'd check in after suppertime, after he had had a chance to take one little look around the town. She said that'd be just fine. And that was why he assumed she had no plans to feed him.

Except she did. She was going to give him breakfast on the days that he was there. He'd stayed in bed until he heard the sounds of someone in the kitchen, and by the time he'd washed and dressed and come down-stairs, he could smell the coffee brewing and the bacon frying—and discovered that she'd set a place for him.

"I wouldn't hold you to my schedule," was the diplo-matic way that Mizzus Beaufort Cartwright made com-pletely sure he knew exactly what the deal was, "so I'll just plan for you to take your lunch and dinner elsewhere. But I'd never let you go out of my house the first thing in the morning without a nice hot break-fast in your stomach."

Over the meal, Phi established he could leave his car right at the curb out front all day, as well as overnight. He told her that the first day, anyway, he'd probably just stroll around. He also let her know the kinds of questions he'd be asking, in hopes that she might tell him who to ask them of and maybe phone ahead for him. To Mr. F. B. Jones, for instance. But she didn't volunteer, unfortunately.

So, by quarter after nine, he left the house, clipboard in hand, already warm inside his father's jacket, but pleased to feel that it, along with his best pair of Dockers and a button-down striped shirt, made him entitled to walk up to *anyone,* and ask him almost anything. Even if he wasn't really eager—motivated—he'd be out there. Hopeful, even if he didn't know for what.

By four o'clock that afternoon, he was wishing that he had that guy from Garston there, and by the throat—the dress-like-the-man-you-want-a-favor-from palooka. That theory was a bust, at least so far. He'd probably approached a half a dozen men with jackets on, and at least another ten who had a jacket folded on their arms or slung over their shoulders—or who had left their jackets hanging in their offices while they went out for lunch or just a coffee.

Almost all of them were very pleasant people, Philo thought, among the nicest adults he had ever met. And many of them had a flair for storytelling and a seemingly encyclopedic memory for events that had occurred in and around Acheron during the most recent half century. The only trouble was that most of the time these stories didn't have a whole lot to do—as far as Phi could see—with (for example) what they'd do if they were starting out again as youngsters, knowing all the stuff that they knew now.

He learned, for instance, that a party by the name of Billy Bob McMartin, back in '87, up and quit his job down at the mill and started pulling copper wire out of the burned-out motors of failed appliances that other people tossed into the dump. This he sold as scrap, and yes, by doing so, he figured out he cleared a good eight cents an hour, even paying nothing for his raw materials. The boy's reaction to all that: So what? Apparently, the point of it was Billy Bob was "happier than pigs in slop," which was not exactly Philo's goal in life.

And, when he asked about their hearts' desires, he learned they mostly wanted still another firearm, or fishing pole, or really fancy pickup—those kinds of things and nothing more . . . substantial. One fellow told a story, answering that question. It seemed, the night before, his wife had called to him when he was watching the TV and told him he should come, and quick, into the kitchen. She was looking through the window there at Walt and Josephine, the next-door neighbors, who, she said, were having just an awful fight. When the fellow looked, himself, he saw the two of them, both armed with brooms and taking mighty swipes at . . . not each other, but a bat! He could see the dang thing swooping through their kitchen. "Bet the one thing them two wanted most," this fellow said, "and didn't have, was one fine *tennis racquet!*" And he laughed delightedly.

The question, though, that hardly got a rise out of anyone at all was the one about "who'd be doing *best,* around here, these days?" As a rule, men said they didn't know, or everyone was simply doing dreadful— or, failing that, they'd just look down at the ground,

154

or off a ways, and mumble something Philo couldn't hear.

Phi couldn't understand this in the slightest. He put it down to ignorance (perhaps), or some depraved kind of jealousy or local weirdness; or it could have been (?) a total lack of interest, or of envy. So he didn't think much of it one way or another when a van pulled up beside him in the parking lot behind the courthouse, and the pleasant-looking woman riding shotgun ran her window down and asked him was it him, by any chance, who wanted information on the subject of the local business climate.

And when he said it was, the big door on the van's right side slid open, and Phi beheld a hugely fat young man, squatting in the dimness of the cargo space. He held the biggest handgun Phi had ever seen, aimed directly at the boy's midsection.

"Get in, bubba," said the man. "Nice and slow, and smile."

Later Philo tried to recollect if it had even crossed his mind to holler. He didn't think it had. For one thing, hollering was not his style. No one in his household was a screamer—except for Marietta, for attention, sometimes. And, secondly, he thought that his companion in the back part of the van would shoot him dead the moment he began to yell, before he got as far as the *l* in "Help! I'm being abducted!" or the first *r* in "Fire! Murder! Rape! Police!"

Shoot him *dead*?

That was borderline unthinkable. Kids in big cities might get shot by accident or by a member of a rival gang. Kids from towns like his did *not* get shot, and when they even *mentioned* dying, there was "boredom" in the sentence, almost always.

He didn't want to die at all. The thought that he might shortly die closed up his throat and robbed him of his will. This was the final reason that he didn't call for help: he couldn't.

As soon as its sliding door slammed shut again, the

van started moving. The fat guy with the big revolver turned on an electric lantern, which did a decent job of lighting up the windowless interior. The van was a custom model, with a wall between the two front seats and back there in the cargo space. There was some kind of padding on the floor, the ceiling, and the sides; probably that made it soundproof, where *he* was. Philo figured *that* out with a shudder. His captor leaned his back against a side wall, squatting in the deep knee-bend position, with his gun hand resting on one massive thigh. He was barefoot, with a Caterpillar cap on and immense bib overalls.

"I think you've made a big mistake," was the sentence that limped out pathetically from Philo's lips when he could finally lick them moist enough to say the words.

"*We* ain't made no big mistake atall," the fat guy answered. "*You* did, when you came and stuck your little tax-supported honker into other people's business."

Phi stared at him; he didn't get it. *Tax-supported honker?* What was that supposed to mean?

"I'm sorry, but I don't know what you mean," he managed to reply. "My name is Philo Fortune; all I am's a high school student. And all that I was trying to do was find myself a good career—something to go into, after college, maybe." He sounded overly polite, he realized—downright nerdy.

"Oh, sure. Yeah. Right," the fat man said. "Nice try. You must think we're really stupid, Fahlo. Sure. *You're* in high school, ain't you? Same as I'm in Nashville, in the Grand Ole Opry."

And for the rest of the trip, everything that Philo said was answered by a shaking of the head and rueful smile. The barrel of the gun, however, stayed completely steady.

From time to time, the fat man got to humming. Phi was sorry that he recognized the song: "The End of the Line."

There were two brief stops before the last one. Both times, one of the people up front got out, walked away, returned, and got back in again.

"That'd be Mama opening up our gate and turning off the *ee*-lectric eye," said Phi's companion, after the first one.

That information added to the boy's discomfort. A gate and an electric eye were not the sorts of things just *anyone* would have. It seemed—the fat guy's Dog-patch outfit notwithstanding—his captors weren't poor. But neither the middle-aged couple in the front seat nor Jumbo with a handgun, here, looked *rich*, like big-time wheeler-dealers, people in their comfort zone. What could the story be? Overall, the gate, this van, and the electric eye suggested they were in some sort of profitable enough business that was possibly illegal. And clearly they believed he was a different person than he was—a spy or, more than likely, some-one from the IRS. Lots of people cheated on their taxes; Philo'd always just assumed he would, some-day—legally, if possible. The question was: Would people kill, for fear of being audited?

The second stop came moments later: that same out-and-in routine; presumably the gate was closed, the magic "eye" reopened. They were almost there, wherever that was. Would it be the place where they were going to . . . rub him out? Phi felt his eyes begin to fill with tears. His family might never learn his fate; he'd become another "missing" kid, another face on a milk carton, a mere statistic. An M.O.A.T.: Missing on a Trip. Marietta'd grow up wondering if she still had a brother out there, somewhere. Thea'd never know, or care, that he had died a few days after she had . . . driven him away. He wished he could have told her . . . lots of things, when he had had the chance.

The van came to another stop. This time, the big side door slid open, and the fat guy said, "Last stop now, bubba. Everybody out."

Phi rubbed his eyes and did as he'd been told. It was very bright outside, and not at all like home, like any Honeysuckle Terrace, anywhere.

This was *country,* and they parked beside a big white house with weathered clapboard sides and shiny, new black vinyl shutters—a remote and rural farmhouse to begin with, but a house that now had . . . well, plantation aspirations, still not totally achieved.

An immense veranda had recently been added to the front of it, supported by six tall white columns, but on the patchy lawn half a dozen geese and one fat pig roamed peacefully and unrestrained. Not far from where he stood was the biggest satellite dish Philo had ever seen, and off one corner of the house was an amazing in-ground pool. It was another custom job, and made to look a great deal like the sort of pool you'd maybe find while hiking in some mountain wilderness (not that Philo ever had). It featured a pipe-fed waterfall, and there were rocks, huge boulders all around it you could dive or jump from. Floating on its surface was a giant rubber crocodile.

A stately weathered barn, as well as other, smaller sheds were all in easy walking distance from the house. One served as a garage, and in it Philo saw a black Mercedes ragtop and a four-door Lexus, gray. Phi started to revise his estimates; it seemed these people *might* be in their comfort zone, or maybe even past it, going up.

The man who'd been their driver walked around in front of him and looked him up and down.

"My, my," he said, "they make 'em younger all the time, I swear." He shook his head, regretfully. "Hate the way this gotta end up for you, sonny, but I s'pose you knew the risks that you was takin'."

This one—presumably the fat man's daddy—was dressed much sharper than his son. He wore a wide-striped shirt—blue and white and buttoned at the neck—and on his head a broad-brimmed Panama hat with a narrow black silk band around it. He looked to Philo like the sort of guy who'd work for Lisa's dad out on the lot, or maybe run a ringtoss game or sell refreshments at a carnival. No matter what he said, he smiled while saying it, and often winked at some point in the sentence. He had a ring that sparkled on his left-hand pinky finger and a sleekly narrow mustache, nicely trimmed.

"No sense not to introduce ourselves," the man went on. "Everything we say will just go with you to your . . . oh, well, never mind." He winked. "Or do you know our monikers already?"

Philo shook his head; he couldn't speak just then. He'd never been an eighth this scared in his entire life. It seemed the fat guy and his father just *assumed* that they were going to kill him.

"Well, fine, if true," the fellow said. "You've met Big Terence, over there, our son and heir. Beside me is Dear Deirdre, who's my loving wife. And *I* am Edwin Yawkey, Senior—Ed, for short. Which also's gonna be the length of time we know each other—short, that is." He smiled and winked again.

Dear Deirdre, curly haired and looking cheerful as a Christmas morning, was an ample woman in an over-size orange T with shoulder pads, and two gold chains around her neck, as well as navy blue culottes and deck shoes without socks. She also smiled and hunched her shoulders up and wiggled fingers at the boy when she was introduced.

Big Terence, on dry land, was even bigger than he'd seemed scrunched up inside the van. He was all of six foot two, or three, but it was the breadth and girth of him that held the boy's attention. His belly was enormous, and his chest as well; even overalls were tight around his watermelon thighs. His big round face was smoothly layered with fat, and in spite of that huge pistol in his hand, he looked to be the sort of person who would lift a Cadillac off a captive local child. (Of course, Phi thought, that didn't mean he wouldn't also shoot a high school kid from out of state.)

"Golly dawg, you know what time it is, already?" Edwin Yawkey, Senior, said. He was consulting his left wrist, on which he wore what could have been a gold Patek Philippe. He turned his head toward Deirdre. "First things first, my dear. Terry gotta eat."

Deirdre beamed at Philo. "Terry eats six times a day," she told him proudly. "Breakfast, brunch, lunch, lunner, dinner—and a bedtime snack. This'd be his lunner, sure enough. Partway between his lunch and dinner."

"Let's hurry and go in, then," said her husband. Terence nodded, motioned with his gun, and Philo followed Ed and Deirdre to the kitchen door and through it, into the big house.

The Yawkey kitchen was another revelation to Philo; it was about three times as big as what he had at home and furnished with the latest from Jenn-Air (six-burner stove, with built-in griddle and two ovens) and Maytag (double-door refrigerator-freezer). There also was a butcher-block table with four great stools around it, and a lot of sliding-glass-doored cupboard space. In addition, there were cages, two of them, hanging from the ceiling, both with doors wide open. In one, and on a perch, there sat a large green parrot who looked up as everyone trooped in.

"Hello," it said, its beady eyes aimed right at Philo. "What's your name?"

"Philo," Philo managed to get out. "Philo Fortune."

"Drop dead," the parrot said, and burst out laughing. All the Yawkeys followed suit.

"Don't mind him," said Deirdre, and she went and stuck her hand inside the cage. "He's a silly-willy, ain't-cha, precious?" The parrot hopped aboard her finger and she brought it right up to her face.

"How's about a kiss, big boy?" she asked the bird. Its neck craned forward and she kissed it, right between the eyes, before she set it down again, this time on her shoulder. Then she bustled over to the icebox and removed a lot of covered Tupperware—five bowls' worth, in fact—all of which she set down in a semicircle at one end of the table.

Meanwhile, Ed had gotten out some plates and knives and forks and glasses, one of which he also filled with milk. Terence took his seat, surrounded by the food, and gave his dad the gun, which he now aimed at Philo.

"Sit down," he told the boy, nodding at the stool beside his son. And, as Philo did, Terence started loading up his plate, making mounds of all the different foods which (if Phi had had to guess) were macaroni salad, sweet potatoes (mashed with minimarshmallows), rice mixed up with fish and spinach, turkey stuffing (corn in it), and coleslaw.

His parents then took single spoonfuls of the coleslaw, clearly more to keep the young man company than anything.

"He'p yourself," Ed Yawkey said to Phi, "if you got any appetite. I don't know that *I* would, sittin' in your shoes."

"He's gonna be a sumo rassler," Deirdre told the boy, and turned her head to beam at Terence. "He saw this piece in *People* magazine, I b'lieve it was, about this great big feller, a Hawaiian boy, who's doin' sumo rasslin' right now, over in Ja-pan, and cleanin' up, I tell you."

"Soon's he saw it," said her husband, "he had, like, a change of life, got himself a goal, you could say. Terry knows we can't do what we're doin' now forever. I'm sure there's smarter guys'n you, up there."

"He's even got a real nice name picked out," said Deirdre. "All them sumo rasslers, they gotta take another name that's just one word. But what our Terry figgered, he could use his own, just jam it altogether with a little different spelling. *Teriyawki*'s what he's gonna call himself, over in Ja-pan. With *i*'s insteada *y*'s. Don't you think that sounds real good?"

Philo nodded, cleared his throat. Here he was, about to die, watching some enormous fat guy stuff his gut and listening to parent-babble.

"I don't mean to change the subject," he began, speaking to the one who seemed to be in charge, if anybody was—Ed Yawkey, Senior. "That is, I *do* mean to, although it's very interesting, about your son."

"I always took to rasslin'," Big Terence now chimed in. "Freestyle, high school rules, behind the barn—it didn't matter none to me. A lot of guys'd give as soon as I got after 'em. An' the way them Japs do oughta be right up my alley. Allus you have to do is push the other fella outa, like, this little bitty *circle* that they got. Push, or heave, or toss, or trip the guy—any way you want. An' I do all of them real good. Once I get a little extra weight on, which I'm doin' now, I oughta be the next thing to unbeatable."

With that he fed himself a mound of food, three quick and heaping forkfuls, probably another pound right there.

"Them Japs won't stand a chance against our boy," his mother said.

Phi felt as if he might be going crazy. It seemed nobody heard—or maybe cared to hear—the things he said. He might as well be dead already. But still, he had to try again.

"Mr. Yawkey, *please*," he said. "Won't you tell me why you brought me here and who you think I am. I mean, I—"

"What I don't see," Ed cut him off, "is why folks can't just lay off, let well enough alone. Live and let live, the way the Good Book tells us to."

"Allus we ever done," Big Terence said, while chewing still more food, "is give the people what they want. Ain't that what cap'talism's all about? The U-S-A-American-type way?"

"We's good, God-fearing people," Deirdre said defensively. "Close-knit as a family but helpful to the needs of others. You can ask anyone."

"Okay, but what I still don't get," said Philo, pleadingly, "is what you want with me—an ordinary high school kid. Or why you'd want to *kill* me, for God's sake."

"Oh, sure," said Mr. Yawkey, Senior, his voice bent out of shape by disbelief. "Some ordinary high school kid *you* are. Who wouldn't have a clue why anyone like us would ever have it in for him. Who never in his life heard tell about the DEA, I guess."

"The DEA?" said Phi. He searched his frightened, cluttered mind. The letters rang a bell that soon became a siren. A story he had read in *Newsweek*, maybe, or in *Rolling Stone* . . . ?

"That's, like, the . . . Drug . . . Enforcement . . . Agency, or something, isn't it?" he said. "You think that *I'm* a *narc*?"

"Know you are," Ed Yawkey, Senior, said. "Ain't no

'think' about it. I got like a sixth sense, passed down from my old daddy and his pa before him—they was in the whiskey bizness. I'da followed in their footsteps, 'cept times changed. But what I'm sayin' is, I get a feelin' from you, boy. It ain't just 'cause you askin' all those damfool questions, Philo. You the *type*."

"The type?" said Philo unbelievingly. "What type is *that*, for God's sake?"

"Goody-goody," Terence answered promptly. "Mama's boy. Me, I got that sixth sense, too. Soon's I saw you, I was sayin' to myself, 'That boy's a snitch.' Straighter'n an arrow, an' maybe half as sharp."

"It don't mean you're evil," Deirdre added philosophically. "This is just the way that some folks are. Lots of 'em are teachers, preachers, and like that."

"Shoot, if I was headin' up the DEA," her husband said, "I'd sign me up a bunch of fellers who looked country. Dumb *and* country, both. Guys you wouldn't look at twice. 'Stead of that, they keep on sending down you straight-and-narrow Yankee kids. You'd think that once they lost a couple, they'd begin to get a clue."

Phi tried to laugh. "Ha-ha-ha-ha," he started—and then gave it up. This wasn't any kind of funny. His captors—unbelievably—were dealing drugs, big time. They thought he was a narc. They'd sized him up as being . . . well, the polar opposite of how he'd always hoped to see himself. They didn't think he was a killer whale, they thought that he was *good*—a goody-goody, even. And, for all those reasons, they now planned on killing him. Was there any earthly way he could stop them?

"Look," he said. "I'm sorry, but you've made a huge mistake. Like I said, my name is Philo Fortune . . ."

The parrot on the woman's shoulder yelled, "Drop dead!" and started laughing, once again.

165

". . . and here"—Phi fished his wallet out—"is my ID card from my high school." He put it on the table, right between the Yawkeys, Senior. "And this is my rental card from the Video Place, and my driver's license, and the registration for my car—it's actually in my mother's name, right there?—and what I'm on is, like, a trip . . ."

He kept on talking, telling them what once upon a time had been his stated reason for going on this trip: his eagerness to find a way to make a lot of money and to have a different lifestyle than the one his parents had. As he listened to himself, he was struck by how much he sounded like some strange suburban version of the Yawkeys, not just in terms of accent, but all around. He didn't mention Thea or the dog, but he did describe his coming into Acheron and meeting Mizzus Cartwright and staying at her home.

"So when you tried to find out who was doin' best in Greater Acheron," said Mr. Yawkey, Senior, when Philo'd finished, "you *wasn't* trying to get the names of who was in the pipeline, here? You tellin' me you didn't even *know* that there was aircraft settin' down in this part of the state, with loads that came from *way* south of the border? You askin' me to think you're only trying to he'p your*self*?"

"Exactly right," said Philo, fitting in like mad. "And lookee here—call up my folks, if you've a mind to. I can give you the number, or you can get it yourself from directory assistance; my daddy's name is Rudyard and my mama's Sarah, and the phone's in both their names. I'll *pay* you for the call. You can ask them if they got a boy named Philo Fortune . . ."

"Drop *dead*," the parrot once again advised him, with a hearty chuckle.

". . . a son in high school, who's away, and on this *trip*," Phi finished.

Nobody answered right away, the only sound in there was Terence chewing.

"If you've got a pen and paper, I could write the number down," said Philo. *"Please."* He'd lost his accent totally. "I'm telling you the *truth*. You call them up. I've got a little sister, Marietta, she might answer, too. You'll see."

Big Terence took another mouthful. Ed and Deirdre looked at one another.

"Sure." Big Terence finally broke the silence. "An' if we make that call, what we'll get'll be another agent, makin' like your daddy or your little sister or your mom. Close, but no see-gar there, Fahlo. We wasn't born exactly *yesterday*, you know."

Shortly after that, when Terry'd finished with his meal, Ed Yawkey, Senior, took Philo downstairs, into the cellar of the house, and locked him in a narrow room that had no windows and only one lightbulb, hanging from a cord. It had a dirt floor and a bunch of shelves along both sides, some of which had canning jars on them.

He felt a little bit relieved. Somehow, he didn't think they planned to kill him in that room; it was more a place for keeping things than for getting rid of them, he thought.

They brought him up again three hours later—he still had his watch on—and offered him some dinner; they were having chili. Phi asked them if they'd called his parents, and the fat guy told him "No!" real fast, like that. The big green parrot wasn't anywhere around, but two gray cockatiels were sitting mutely in the other open cage. Neither Ed nor Deirdre spoke to him, other than to offer food, and every other question that he asked was met by shrugs from all of them.

167

When they had finished eating, Ed Yawkey, Senior, took Philo to the bathroom and then back downstairs. Someone had set a cot up in his "room" while he was in the bathroom and put a blanket and a pillow on it. Beside the cot, resting on the earthen floor, there was a big black iron ball with a chain attached to it and a single handcuff attached to the chain.

Ed Yawkey, Senior, made the boy undress and hand him all his clothes. Then he snapped the handcuff onto Phi's left wrist, unscrewed the lightbulb from its socket, left the room, and closed and locked the door.

"If you get out and try to run," were his departing words, "I doubt you'll go real far. That ball weighs fifty pounds, and one thing we got plenty of, down here, is snakes."

20

Lying naked in the darkness, handcuffed to some fifty pounds of metal weight, Philo simply tried to keep himself from losing it, at first. He'd read somewhere that that could happen. To a convict thrown in solitary, put down in the hole. He was pretty sure he'd read that some guys couldn't take it, that they got hysterical and yelled and screamed—went nuts.

He told himself to think about his situation very calmly, analytically. So it was really dark in there. Well, he was used to that. It was pitch-dark in his room at home, at night. He wanted it that way. His mom had gone to Ames and gotten special shades and put them on his windows for him. *(Mama's boy?)* That way, he could sleep late on weekends. So he was used to total darkness. He never got the urge to turn a light on in his room at home, at night; why should he want to, here? It didn't matter that he *couldn't* have a light on, here. He didn't *need* one on, no way.

He was naked, but that, too, was not peculiar. In the summertime especially, at home, he'd sometimes sleep that way. Some people always did, he'd read, and some of them were movie stars and models, females with fantastic bodies. The whole idea of sleeping in the nude was pretty sexy. Not tonight, perhaps, but other times, in general. And anyway, he had a blanket there that he could cover up with, if he wanted. *(Goody-goody?)*

The handcuff and the iron ball *were* new to him. There wasn't any getting around that. But the chain was long enough so that his handcuffed hand could be up on the bed, right near his chest, as usual. Turning over would be . . . difficult, but heck, he didn't toss and turn much, as a rule.

The fact (if it was even true) that there were snakes outside was totally irrelevant. He wasn't going to go outside, and there was no way snakes could slither in the house, like . . . through the cellar walls, or something. And then get on that iron ball and climb right up the chain . . .

He kneeled up on his cot and, pulling on the chain, lifted up the heavy ball and set it on the bed, beside him. That proved to be uncomfortable, however, having the great weight of it right there, rolling toward and pressing on his chest.

And it was silly, too. There weren't any snakes in his small room. He kneeled up again and dropped the iron ball onto the floor. It *thunked* onto the floor—it didn't *squish.* He picked it up a few more times and dropped it all around the cot. Every time, it thunked. There weren't any snakes in there.

He lay back down and found that if he listened really hard, he could hear a TV on, upstairs. He couldn't tell which program; all he heard was a murmuring and sometimes music. But it *was* TV, and that was sort of homelike, oddly comforting.

Suppose he *did* die (he began to think). Suppose the Yawkeys killed him. It was a hard thing to imagine:

being shot, for instance. Would it feel like anything, a bullet ripping through his brain? But suppose he did get killed. What then? What could be said about his life; what did his seventeen-plus years add up to? Suppose he had to give himself a grade on them—what would it be?

If he was going to be completely honest (and he decided that he should be, given his predicament), and he couldn't take an Incomplete, he figured he was worth about a C.

Or . . . make that a B minus. No point in overgroveling; he wasn't all *that* bad.

But the truth was: he couldn't claim to have accomplished much, so far. At school, he got good grades all right, but so did lots of people. And if his world at school was just a stage, he was cast only in bit parts or in crowd scenes. Granted that he hung around, at times, with perfectly nice-looking girls—but they were just supporting players, too. The girls who had their names in lights at school were not for him. They only went with leading men, the superstars. He didn't have a cool Miata or a muddy, loaded Jeep to tool around in; he was the Squareback man. He was known to be ambitious and to have a lot of future plans, but anyone could *talk.*

No, in the artificial world of high school, he was one of many, a member of the middle class.

In the *real* world, though, he seemed to come across as even worse. Thea'd made no bones about her . . . well, *contempt* for what he'd come to think of as his killer-whale-to-be routine. In fact, it even seemed as if she'd seen . . . oh, through it (or *beyond* it?), to a person she could care about and wanted to be with, until . . .

And these Yawkeys here, who'd barely *met* him—they had reached their own unflattering (but maybe similar) conclusions. They said he was a goody-goody

171

and a mama's boy. The way they sized him up, he wouldn't ever be an entrepreneur. In their eyes, he was absolutely not the sort of person who would show initiative and take a lot of risks—who'd devote himself to getting rich off other people. No, they had him figured for the kind who'd try to throw the killer whales in jail!

Finally, there was how his parents saw him. Well (he thought), they loved him and believed in him, all right. They really did; he *knew* that. But who, exactly, was it they believed in?

He thought (no, hell, he knew) it wasn't the kid who talked about his comfort zone and incredible annual income. They probably believed in someone a lot . . . *simpler* than that. Like the guy who'd sat there in that motel and told Thea how much he loved and (yes!) admired them. The one who (therefore) certainly had *tendencies* to be a goody-goody and a mama's boy.

He wondered if his parents knew (as Thea did) the way he really felt about them. If not, that'd be a major shame, like a catastrophe, almost. He'd stressed his money-grubbing side with them (he now realized) because it seemed important to proclaim that he was different from the way they were, in ways that went beyond . . . oh, listening to music, say. If he appeared to be a clone of theirs, it'd be the same as, well, admitting he was still a *child,* incapable of thinking for himself, of having ideas of his own. He'd wanted them to be a little mystified by him. He'd hoped they wouldn't always "understand."

But if he was going to die, he hoped his parents really *had* seen through him and had known that he was jiving (lots of times) and, deep down, thought that they were wonderful. (If he survived . . . well, he could think about that later.)

172

He also had the same hope with respect to Thea, though in her case it was pretty faint. He'd been such an idiot with her, so much of the time: making judgments, showing off, erupting out of underbrush, trying to be a macho man. She'd seemed to have forgiven him a lot of that—or refused to believe it, better. But at the end, when she'd reached out to him, he'd let her down. He hadn't been mature enough, or sensitive enough, to help her; his reaction to her story added up to, simply, *more abuse.* He'd told her only once that he loved her, and never why, how much—in full, true, glorious detail.

He wondered if perhaps the Yawkeys might allow him to write letters, just before . . . the end. One to his folks and Marietta, another one to Thea. Instead of a last meal. Not that Thea'd ever get hers. He didn't know her last name, or where she was from, or where she was going. She was almost like a dream—mysterious like that (as well as hurt and virtuous and beautiful). And if he wasn't such an idiot, she might have been *his* dream come true, and he'd be with her now, nowhere near this cellar, nowhere near . . . the end.

Good God (he thought); the reason he was going to *die* was that he'd failed as Thea's friend. That he'd run away, just fled, instead of facing up to, dealing with, a . . . messy situation. This wasn't any killer-whale-to-be; he'd acted like a frightened minnow.

He began to feel acutely sorry for himself. For him to have to die, right then, seemed totally unfair. He might have had a great life as the kind of person he now thought he either *was* or wanted to become: a mature and loving, truthful and courageous character. Major corporations, old-line Wall Street law firms *looked* for guys like that to bring on board. And later, somewhere up the line, public office might have proved to be a real attractive option for him.

And if, by some amazing miracle, he could have tracked down Thea, somehow, and she'd given him another chance . . .

Thinking that turned out to be too much. In spite of all his good intentions, he became a little boy again, furious at forces—this time, the Yawkeys with their snakes and guns—that he could not control. And *miserable* he wasn't going to get his way and see his dreams come true: a perfect sex (and even married) life, while living in a new, improved (and, face it, even higher) comfort zone.

It was at that point in the night that Philo Fortune— new, improved, unrecognized, and unappreciated— lost it and began to cry.

"Awright, Fahlo honey, tahm to rahz and shahn," was how he heard Dear Deirdre's wake-up call as she came down the cellar stairs.

He sat up straight in bed, inside the pitch-dark cell, uncertain for a moment where he was. The handcuff on his wrist reminded him. He realized he was naked, and he groaned as she unlocked the door.

"Gonna be another scorcher," Deirdre said. She screwed the lightbulb back into its socket. "There we go."

Philo blinked, then rubbed his eyes with his free hand. It had been the worst night of his life, by far, no contest. He was still alive, but only barely (he'd have told his mom, if he had been at home). He didn't think he'd slept for more than half an hour.

"Let's get you off that mean ol' ball," said Deirdre, bending to unlock the handcuff. "That's much better, isn't it? Now come along upstairs and have some breakfast. Terry's halfway done, already."

He swung a leg down off the cot, then pulled it back again.

"I need my clothes," he said.

"Your *clothes*?" she echoed. She made it sound as if she'd never heard the word before. "I don't believe I recollect what Mr. Yawkey said he did with any *clothes*. Better you just wrap that blanket, there, around you and come up. He's run out on an errand; no tellin' when he might be coming back."

"What time is it?" said Philo, wrapping, doing as she'd said. Anything to leave that little room, the night he'd had in there.

" 'Bout a quarter after nine," she told him cheerfully. "We don't keep early hours, since we gave up growin' corn for profit."

Upstairs in the kitchen, Phi found Terry sitting at the same place by the kitchen table that he'd occupied the day before. Clearly, he was breakfasting—on flapjacks, sausage, corn bread, syrup, scrambled eggs, dry cereal with milk and fruit, and coffee.

All three birds—the parrot and both cockatiels— were also on the table. (From time to time one of them would lunge at Terry's plates and beak a bite of food—they all liked scrambled eggs—and that would cause another one to shout *"uh-*oh!" and Mrs. Y. to say, "You naughty boy" and giggle.)

" 'Morning, Fahlo," Terry mumbled affably, corn bread crumbs at either corner of his mouth. That day, he had a T-shirt and green work pants on, the pistol jammed down in the waistband of the trousers.

"How about some eggs and bacon?" Deirdre asked Philo. "Won't take but a minute. He'p yourself to juice there, in the fridge."

Philo couldn't see why not. He was pretty hungry, actually, which proved that he was still alive.

"Thank you very much," he said, picking up the empty glass from where he'd sat before. As he passed the kitchen window, something outside caught his eye. A car. A Squareback. His.

"My car!" he said, as if it were a long-lost friend.

"Yep," said Terry. "Collected 'er last night. Dad took me over an' I drove 'er back. Not much pickup in them Squarebacks, is there?"

Of course, Phi thought; when they took his clothes, they'd got his car keys, too. And he'd told them where he'd stayed the night before.

"You went and stole my *car*?" he said.

"Goodness gracious no," said Deirdre, busy by the stove. "We Yawkeys ain't no *thiefs.* Never was and never will be."

"We visited a bit with Mizzus Cartwright," Terry said. "She was glad to hear that you was going to stop with us a while, and have some country livin' while you're at it."

"Mr. Yawkey said *she* said you was a real nice boy," said Deirdre as she dropped some bacon slices on the griddle. "Said you had the manners of a preacher, Mr. Yawkey said. Just like I *saids*, what I told Mr. Yawkey."

"I suppose you told her that I'd *given* you the keys, and you were doing me a *favor*," Philo said to Terry, feeling surly, sleep-deprived.

"Got *that* right," said Terry, offering the big green parrot one more bite of flapjack. "Told her you was plumb wore out from asking all those questions all day long. But you don't have to worry. I told her thankee for you—an' good-bye."

Philo's stomach did a flip. Partly from the smell of bacon frying—turned out he really was ravenous again—and partly . . . well, because that last bit made him feel the Yawkeys had passed sentence on him, in absentia. That he, and all his worldly goods, were getting set to . . . disappear.

"What happens next?" he had to ask—even knowing that he might not want to know. He didn't feel too much like writing letters, at that moment. Maybe, once he'd eaten breakfast, he would ask.

"You *eat*, I guess," said Terry with a shrug. "After that . . . well, Daddy ought to be back soon."

Moments later, Mrs. Yawkey put a heavy plate in front of Phi. Five perfect strips of bacon, scrambled eggs with buttered toast, no grits—a Yankee breakfast, even. Then she was back again, with coffee. The three birds started walking up and down in front of him, back and forth across the table, looking at his plate from time to time and muttering.

Phi had to eat. Because it smelled and looked so good, to keep his strength up, and in order to have something else to think about. If this was Southern hospitality, it wasn't overrated; he'd never had a better breakfast in his life. He kept an arm between it and the tropical marauders.

When he was done, he shook his head and even smiled at Terry Yawkey. "Your mom, she sure can cook," he said.

"Tell me about it," said the fat man, playing bongos on his belly.

Philo (desperate mama's boy and lacking any other cards to play) got the blanket cinched around his waist, took his dishes to the sink, and started washing them. And that was where he was when Terry's dad pulled up outside, driving their big van. Two minutes later he walked in the kitchen door.

"I stopped down by the health food store," he told his son, "an' had a real good parley with that feller there. He told me with the diet he laid out, including special herbs, and doing healthful exercise, you *could* be two-oh-five and feelin' fine inside of two months' time. I left the stuff I got from him out on the porch.

All kindsa things, from apple juice to rice cakes down to *kelp*, which is some kind of seaweed. Figgered you could horse it in when you've a mind to."

"Well, thankee, Daddy," Terence said.

Philo looked perplexed. "I don't understand,"—he couldn't help but stick his oar in there—"I thought the idea was for Teriyawki to *gain* weight." He waved a hand at all the plates there on the table.

"*Was*," Ed Yawkey, Senior, said. "Most likely, was. We got a new idea we're workin' on." He winked, then paused and looked uneasy. "Called your mama up, you see. Yesterday afternoon, when you was first down cellar."

Philo inhaled sharply, felt his heart begin to pound. They'd made the call, talked to his mom! Could she have fixed things up? Again? As usual? He didn't dare to ask, to speak. Ed Yawkey, Senior, sat down. Clearly, he had more to say.

"Fact is, we believe—we now believe—you're who you said you was," Ed Yawkey, Senior, said. "A gah-damn high school kid, out on a gahdamn trip." He chuckled then, and shook his head, and tried to look disgusted.

"Me, I'm *glad* you're not an agent with the DEA," Dear Deirdre said. "I never *liked* you bein' one of them atall."

Phi took another real deep breath and spoke to all of them at once, although he didn't look at anyone. He tried to loll back on his stool (almost falling over backward in the process) and sound offhand, and calm, and confident.

"So," he said. "I guess that means I'm free to go. Mrs. Yawkey"—now he did look at her husband—"said you'd put my clothes somewhere. If I could have them back, them and my wallet and my keys, I really should be on my—"

"What I told your mama was, I was the Cuthbert County sheriff," said Ed Yawkey, Senior, interrupting, sounding pleased, "an' that I'd found you sleeping in that Squareback out behind the new consolidated high school. She swallowed that one, hook an' line an' sinker." Then he nodded, laughing now. "I said that I was checking to make sure you hadn't *stole* that fine old car of hers."

"Right," said Philo, chuckling along with him, butter-basting him with laughter. He had the feeling, once again, he wasn't being paid attention to.

"She couldn't have described you any better, short of sending us a pitcher of you bareass on a bearskin rug," Terry's dad went on. "An' she explained the purpose of your trip as best she could. But most of all, she sounded real authentic, like your *mama.* No way any agent could have faked that up."

Phi blushed. With pleasure? In a way. Good old Mom. He'd pay her back for this, for sure, somehow. He started to stand up, forgetting he had just a blanket (which had come undone) around his waist. He blushed some more and quickly sat back down again, as all three birds, Terry, and Dear Deirdre had themselves a case of mild hysterics.

"Well. So," he said again, when they had quieted, "I thank you for . . . your hospitality. And now if I could just—"

"Forget it, Fahlo," said Ed Yawkey, Senior. "You ain't goin' *no*where at the moment, knowing what you do."

Mr. Yawkey spelled out what he called "the horns of mah die-lemma." On the one hand, if Phi wasn't a federal agent, he didn't see how he could "conscientiously put two, three extra holes" in him. But on the other hand, now that the boy'd become aware of what was going on out at the Yawkey farm, he didn't see how he could let him live.

"We been thinkin' on it all night long," he told the boy. "We got a world-class problem."

"How can you kill and *not* kill the same guy?" said Terry. "That's the fifty-dollar question."

"For all our sakes," Dear Deirdre said, "there's got to be an answer."

This time, Philo looked at each of them, in turn. Even Mr. Yawkey now looked solemn like the others, solemn and concerned; it seemed that everyone was thinking, hard as he or she was able. He decided he had better join them fast. This was the kind of thing that was—or used to be—his kind of challenge: finding the impossible—and bold—alternative, a way around the problem, a route to use to weasel out.

How could he guarantee that if the Yawkeys let him go, he'd never tell on them? If he could find the answer to that question, he might yet survive.

He stood up, this time with the blanket tight around his waist, held there by one hand.

"Is it all right for me to use . . . ," he gestured toward the bathroom, not sure what to call it. "The john" seemed awfully Honeysuckle Terrace.

"Go on ahead," said Mr. Yawkey. "But if you think to jump on out the window, lemme tell you that'll set the geese to honkin' and myself to comin' at you, with that gun."

Philo hadn't even thought of trying to escape. The idea of running through the heated brushy haze of Acheron, clutching at a blanket round his waist, while looking out for snakes, was quite unthinkable. He had other, more traditional ideas concerning what he'd do there, in the bathroom.

And sure enough, five minutes later he emerged to say, "I've got it—the solution!"

Three heads snapped up, Dear Deirdre looking proud of him, he thought, the other two at least attentive.

"How about you let me *work* for you a while?" said Philo. "I'd do anything you say—the more against the law, the better. I'll even sign a written contract, saying I voluntarily agree to work for you in . . . let me see, in any and all aspects of the illegal drug trade—for whatever you wanted to pay me a week. Except you wouldn't have to pay me anything, of course. Then, after a few weeks—or whatever you say—you could let me hop right in my car and go! I could call my parents up right now and tell them I was working on a farm, for room and board, for the *experience.* They'd *love* to hear that I was doing that, I guarantee you."

Ed Yawkey, Senior, pursed his lips. Big Terence nodded, indicating understanding, Philo felt. But, just in case . . .

"Of course you get my point," the boy continued. "If I'm guilty of the same things you are, I'd be *nuts* to ever turn you in."

Ed Yawkey, Senior, shook his head and did that laugh of his again. "That's really not half bad," he said. "Except for two main things. Number one,"—he held a finger up—"you may *be* nuts, for all we know. And number two,"—his middle finger joined the first one—"there's just no way that you could *do* the same things we been doin'. And you'd have to do 'em, and in front of witnesses. A written contract don't mean diddly."

"What?" said Philo. "Why couldn't I do the same as you? I know I'm not as big and strong as Terry is, but I'm no weakling, either. Try me out; you'll see. I keep in shape at home, no kidding."

"Not talkin' physical can-do," Mr. Yawkey said. "What I mean is more along the lines of *attitude.* It's just like Terry said—you a goody-goody, right? You ain't got this kind of nonsense in your genes, the same way we do."

As Philo started to protest, Mr. Yawkey held a hand

up. "No use tellin' me you took a lotta change from Mama's handbag, as a little kid, or that you sell your homework answers to the loafers at your school," he said. "I purely don't believe that you're the type to break the law—commit a federal offense. When push got up to shove, you'd find you couldn't get yourself to do it, which—let me tell you something—ain't all bad. That's what my sixth sense tells me, boy.

"And anyways, an' like I said," he finished, "there's this other small idea we've all been workin' on."

Although deflated and depressed, when Philo heard the "small idea," he had to give the Yawkeys credit. That is, his *old self* would have had to give the Yawkeys credit. His *new* self—or at least the self he'd thought, the night before, he might well have become, or had been, really, all along—admired only part of what he heard. That was the first part of this small idea.

According to Ed Yawkey, Senior, Deirdre and he were thinking—*had* been, for some time—of giving up their "lahf of crahm," the drug biz.

"We been readin' up on what this product does to folks," he told the boy. "An' how the gov'mint ain't doing squat to he'p the ones who turn to it, on accounta they so mizzuble to start with."

"Possibly they will, someday," said Deirdre, "but it sure ain't happened yet."

"The DEA and them keep thinkin' they can cut off the supplah," her husband said. "They're full of it, I say. Folks are too damn shiftless, too damn greedy, an' there's too much open space out there. I don't care if you mean here or California or some other state, or down there in Peru or Mexico, Colombia, or one of them. As long as there's good money to be made, better money than a guy can make just plantin'

183

corn or sloppin' hogs—or workin' at some burger joint—gahs are gonna go for it. Take us, for an example."

"At first," Dear Deirdre said, "we figgered it was just about like makin' whiskey, which both our families been doin' since the dawn of time. Except it paid a whole lot better. We didn't use what we was sellin', so we didn't know a whole hell of a lot about it. Way we saw it, we was just in business, still. Hush-hush, sure enough,"—she made a wiggle-waggle motion with one hand—"but hell, we had that in our blood. The way folks look at it down here, sellin' hootch and bein' smarter than the G-men is a kind of local recreation— a *tradition* even, you might say."

"But when we started readin' up a little on this new stuff we've been movin'," said Ed Yawkey, Senior, "that's when she an' me began to have these second thoughts. And third and fourth on top of them. We also saw we had a lotta dollars set aside, more'n we could ever use, in fact. On top of that, this place is worth a pretty penny."

"Not to mention," Deirdre added, "maybe we'd decide to sell the business—contacts and goodwill, that kinda thing—an' make another pile, though chances are we'd simply close 'er up and walk away. With all that cash, we'd just take off. Have ourselves one long vacation, right up to the gates of everlastin'. There's lotsa things we always said we'd like to go and see— that Stonehenge over there, an' how about them pyramids?—but never did, hard as we been workin' all our lives."

"The one thing she and me was bothered by," said Ed, "was Terry, here; how this might stick a booger in his plans. She'n me, we figgered we could change our names, identities and all, and more or less, like, *disappear*. But Terry, here, if he went into rasslin', he'd be a public *figger.* Questions would get asked 'bout who he was and where he come from. Once he started beatin' up on Japanese, they probably might send *reporters* over here to nose round and see what kinda dirt they might dig up on him. You put a thousand-dollar bill in front of certain ones in Acheron (an' I ain't namin' names), an' they'd sing songs concerning anything they'd seen since poppin' outa mama's belly."

"But what my daddy and my mama didn't know," said Terry, picking up the talk with relish, "was I was gettin' dreadful sick of bein' *fat.* A girl I wanted to go out with awful bad, she told me I was gross and always would be gross, even if I got to be the sumo champion of all the world. But I still kept putting on like I was gonna be it, 'cause I didn't want to disappoint my folks. So, just last night, they told me what all they'd been thinking, and how much in cold hard cash would come my way if we sold out . . . ," he paused to beam at both his parents, ". . . an' I just hollered, 'Golly *dawg*—I'm goin' on a dict, startin' after breakfast.' "

He turned around to Philo and he winked, the way his daddy had. "With that brand-new shape of mine," he said, "and bein' rich as hell, girls oughta pitch a tent and get in line to date me, doncha think? 'Stead of gettin' me a big ol' piece of chicken two, three times a day, I'll pick and choose a little juicy p—"

"Terry!" Deirdre cut him short, beaming same as usual. "You watch what you be sayin', now." She turned to Phi. "But yes, his daddy and myself were mighty pleased to hear how much he went for our idea."

Philo nodded, but his mind was elsewhere. What he hadn't heard was any further mention of *his* situation. Would he get liquidated, too, along with all their other

185

assets? Or, once they packed their bags and got their airline tickets, might they just leave him in a swamp someplace (while heading to the airport, say) and let him find his own way out—and home?

He cleared his throat and tried to frame a gentle, useful question.

"Just out of curiosity," he said, "where do I—"

Ed Yawkey, Senior, hit the chuckle button. "Why, you're another one of our assets," he explained, "worth a week at Monte Carlo, everything first class, an' high-stakes blackjack every night. We gonna hold your little butt for ransom."

Kidnapped! thus became the latest word to bang some pots and pans around in Philo's nervous system. Before, it seemed as if he was a target, plain and simple, and was going to be rubbed out. But he'd escaped that fate, thanks to his quick thinking, and his credible, supportive mom. Only to achieve this other awful status: kidnap victim.

"Oh no," he muttered. Not being (1) a capo in the Mafia, or (2) the son of anybody rich or famous (or that somebody himself), he'd never thought he'd be held for ransom.

And of the kidnap victims he could think of—the Lindbergh baby, Patty Hearst, and some millionaire he'd read about—only one had managed to survive: the *female.*

"Look," he told Ed Yawkey, Senior, and his wife and son, "that's really not a doable idea. My parents don't have any money. That's the very thing that's *wrong* with them."

"They may not *have* a lot of money," Terry said, "but betcha they could get their hands on some."

"Thing is," Deirdre offered, "love *is* money. That's why Terry's right."

Love is *money*? That was a concept Phi had never heard before. What did she mean by that? He'd loved his parents and his sister, but he'd never fancied he was rich.

"I guess you think that love is just as *good* as money," he came out with.

"Well, sure, but more than that," she said. "I mean, it's currency, the same as money is. A person, he can waste it, spend it, or invest it, just the same as you can do with cash. An' iffen you invest it wisely, well, you're gonna get a whole lot back."

"Huh," said Philo noncommittally. He wondered if he might be cracking up again. Some things the Yaw-keys said were sounding, if not wise, at least not dumb. Loving his parents had produced, in addition to a lot of other things, this trip. Loving Thea—even kind of half-assedly—had won him her companion-ship, as well as chances for lots more.

"Bein' in love's like being rich, except it's even bet-ter," Terry then observed (apparently inspired to phi-losophize). "Makes you think there's nothing you can't do. You could pass right through a needle's *ah,* ridin' on a camel, like the Good Book says."

"Huh?" said Philo again. He would have liked to tell the fat guy not to press his luck, to stick to . . . oh, conspicuous consumption. But that would not be him—the *new* him—as he was then.

"Or lookee here," said Ed. "Take credit cards. Let's say a person has a credit card, but not a nickel in the bank. Every time he signs a charge slip, he puts every blessed thing he owns and loves right on the line, ain't that the truth? He uses love like money *then,* I hope to tell ya. An' he's shootin' craps with both of them."

"Yeah, right. But anyway," said Phi, before the virus struck again, "let's just suppose my folks can't raise the ransom that you want. What happens then? And how much is it that you're asking for?" He shook his head, now feeling pretty agitated.

"Haven't even asked yet," Terry answered. "As of now, they still don't know their boy's been snatched. There's lotsa details that we gotta get worked out. We're still dottin' *ahs* an' crossin' *tees.*" He smirked.

"I gotta feeling that they'll find a way to get the cash we ask 'em for," Dear Deirdre said. "I know I would, if *I* was them and you was you."

"Woop-woop." That was Ed Yawkey, Senior, standing now and peering out the window. "Looks like we got ourselves a visitor."

"Who is it, Ed?" his wife inquired. "Want that I should warm the coffee up?"

" 'Don't believe so," he replied. "It's one I never seen before." By this time, Terry'd joined him at the window.

"What's he doin' out there?" Deirdre asked.

"She," said Terry. "It's a *she.* She's lookin' at ol' Fahlo's car."

"I'll go out," his father told him. "Chances are she's from some church or other. But pass me that there Magnum, son, for just in case. If Fahlo starts to peep, you touch him with that iron frying pan."

Terry gave his dad the big revolver, watched him stick it down his waistband in the back and head on out the door. Then he *did* pick up the round black fry pan from the stove; he held it resting on his shoulder, much as if it were a caveman's club.

"You stay put," he said to Philo who, in fact, was frozen to his stool.

"What's going on now, son?" Deirdre asked, sipping at her mug of coffee.

"Well, she's showin' Daddy something on a big white sheet of paper," Terry said. "Could be some kinda map or deed; I just can't tell from here. Allus I can see's the back of it. She's got a real fine-lookin' big ol' dog with her, I guess—and mah-mah-mah, she ain't so bad, herself."

Philo tried to think of anything to say or do that might disguise his feelings at that point in time. A real fine-lookin' big ol' dog? A girl who ain't so bad, herself? Who rated a mah-mah-mah?

"Polly want a cracker?" he said softly to the birds, hoping that would come across as epochal indifference to the goings-on outside. The parrot shook its head at him, perhaps disgusted by his unoriginality.

"She keeps pointin' at the car and noddin'," Terry said. "Looks like Daddy's bringin' her inside."

He knew it would be Thea, would have bet the ranch on that. And so a part of him was up there floating in the skinny air, the highest sky, checking out the ozone layer, way on past ecstatic. She'd followed him, *come after him.* She'd remembered where he'd said he planned to go and had found a way to get there fast. Apparently, it *had* been Genie he had seen back in that service area; the two of them had almost beat him down to Acheron!

But he'd barely zoomed up to those heights of joy when he came crashing down again. Look what she'd gotten into, thanks to him! Whatever fate befell him, she was going to end up sharing it.

Oh God (he thought), there was a sentence that he (very shortly) ought to say: "Just let the girl go, and I'll . . . *something.*"

But he didn't know—could not imagine—what that "something" ought to be. He had a parrot and two cockatiels there on the table, right in front of him, but not a single chip that he could bargain with.

The door swung open and she walked into the Yawkeys' kitchen, saw him sitting at the table, there.

She stopped, her eyes real wide and looking at his bare, and not that hairy, unscarred chest.

["Then you're all right?" she said. "I didn't . . . ?"]

He stood up.

["Oh, no. No, just a tiny scratch. But I—," he said. "What I did was the total pits, leaving you like that, the worst thing that I've ever done. I'm so completely, truly sorry. I'm the rotten bastard of all time—"]

["It was my fault," she insisted. "Getting drunk like that. Going crazy over nothing. How else could you have looked, when I'd just dropped a load that size on you . . . ? You'd actually been great, all afternoon—"]

["Uh-uh," said Philo. "I completely let you down. I acted like a total baby—couldn't handle something real and major, something more significant than making money or, or . . . the SATs. And then I ran away, abandoned you. Talk about a total lack of virtue—"]

["Shut up," she said. "Don't talk that way about the person that I love . . ."]

They started smiling at each other.

["Oh, God—I can't believe this. I love you. I have since I first picked you up. How did you ever—"]

["Look." She nodded at the paper in her hand. "I drew your picture, just from memory. It's perfect. People recognized you. A man sent me to Mrs. Cartwright's house, and she sent me out here."]

He took the four quick steps and wrapped his arms around her. She hugged him back, completely joyfully (it felt like). Though neither of the two had said a word since she'd come into the room, no witness to the scene could fail to grasp its meaning.

"Seems like they know each other," Deirdre said, and she was beaming. "Like each other, too."

Thea turned to look down at the dog, who'd just been standing by the two of them, wagging her long tail.

"It's *Philo,* Genie—look!" she said, holding the boy by both his upper arms and shaking him a little. "It's Philo, our old *friend!*"

She turned to Deirdre Yawkey. "I got so excited when I saw his car outside your house," she said, "I started jumping up and down." She shook her head, laughing at herself.

Phi didn't think he'd ever seen her quite so beautiful. She wore her purple cap, as usual, now pushed back on her head, her hair all stuffed inside. Her skin was smooth as flower petals; her eyes the color of deep ocean water on a perfect summer day. She looked a little dazed and wholly carefree, like the winner of a record-setting giant lotto game.

"So," she said to Philo, "Mrs. Cartwright said you planned to stay out here a day or two? D'you think your friends'd mind,"—she looked around at Deirdre, Ed, and Terry—"if I camped out here until you're set to go? Maybe"—she turned back to Phi—"we could take a little drive right now, and let them talk that idea over." She started laughing. "After you get dressed, I mean. My gosh, I didn't even notice . . . What's that—a *sarong?*" She covered up her mouth, still laughing at his blanket-wrap.

That was the last laugh anybody laughed for quite some time. Many hours later, Philo tried to figure out a true chronology, an accurate accounting of what happened next, and after that, and after *that,* and so on. But with all those animals and people playing parts, it really wasn't easy. To get it all entirely straight, to *say.*

Probably the first two minutes after Thea asked if he was wearing a sarong were the very most confused and action packed of all. These things seemed to happen very close together:

—Philo started saying, "Well, the thing is . . ."

—The parrot and the cockatiels, in wedge formation, sped across the table toward a final scrap of food (some corn bread?) still on one of Terry's plates, and in the process sent the syrup pitcher and the plate that held the butter crashing to the floor.

—Ed Yawkey, Senior, also in reply to Thea, dragged the pistol from his waistband (in the back). "Hate to spoil your day, young lady," he began, pointing it at her, "but neither one of you's about to take . . ."

—There was the sound of heavy footsteps on the porch, outside the window, followed by some grunts and snarfling.

—Deirdre Yawkey, hearing that, rose from her stool and headed for the window, probably to try to put a stop to what she had a good idea was happening outside.

—Thea stood there trying to take in everything, to *understand*, looking at, in order, Mr. Yawkey's gun, the mess down on the floor, and back again at Philo.

—Deirdre, on her second step, landed squarely on the butter, lost her balance altogether, and fell forward. Doing so, and quite by chance, she executed what the football people call a cut or crack-back block, this one on/against her king-size son.

—Terry, belted by his falling mother's shoulder on the outside of his knee, spun around and started to go down, his legs knocked out from under him.

—The birds took off and flew across the room, while crying out all three of them, *"Uh*-oh! *Uh*-oh! *Uh*-oh!"

—As Terry flung his arms out, trying to recover his balance, he swung the frying pan around and accidentally bopped poor Thea on her purple baseball cap.

You could, as Philo later did, call that the final action in act 1.

As act 2 started, Philo dropped down on one knee, trying to succor his beloved, who was clearly quite unconscious, on the floor.

At the same time he was going down, Deirdre (unaware of Thea's accidental bopping, the noise of Terry's falling having covered that) got up on her feet again and made it to the window with a muttered "sorry, Sonny," opened it, and stuck her head and shoulders out. Phi could hear her yelling something on the order of "G'wan! Hey, scat! You get your damn snout outa there!"

Ed Yawkey, Senior, hearing her, did that "woop-woop" of his again, followed by, "I reckon that I shouldn'a left ol' Terry's health food stuff out there."

"I guess you shouldn't," Deirdre said. "Looks to me as if the sow got in his seaweed. I b'lieve she ate it all."

Philo, cradling his honey in his arms, became aware of movement on the other side of her. Genie, who'd been sitting on her haunches, looking down at Thea, seemingly concerned, had gotten to her feet and now was focusing on Deirdre.

"What's that?" said Terry to his mom. "Gahdamn, you did a number on my leg, you know that, Mama?" He came up off the floor, holding his left knee. "What's that that you was sayin'?"

"The sow got in the seaweed," Deirdre said, distinctly.

And all hell broke loose.

Segue to act 3.

Neither Philo nor the others in the room (including Thea, with her eyes closed, unresponsive still) had ever seen the likes of what occurred then, in the Yawkey kitchen.

In fact, few people anywhere have had that privilege (or real bad luck, depending on one's point of view) to see a CIA-trained dog in action. Some Secret Service trainers in Virginia have been witnesses, of course—being the ones who taught the animals in the first place. So have certain agents in the field and (to their great regret) members of the KGB, Middle Eastern terrorism teams, and others dangerous to U.S. national security.

In Secret Service lingo, all the things that Genie did in the course of the next forty-five seconds or so of act 3 are known, collectively, as AD-BAG, for *Attack Disarm—Bring Ally Gun.*

She launched herself, initially, at Mr. Yawkey, getting her strong jaws around his wrist and chomping down, causing him to yelp in pain and drop the gun. Then, by growling fiercely (with her lips retracted) and, to even more effect, snapping at their crotches, she caused both Ed and Terry to move back, quite quickly, into Deirdre, making the three of them a single mass of terrified Attacked, Disarmed humanity.

Then, turning quickly, she retrieved the big revolver from the floor and trotted with it in her mouth toward Philo—dropping it, in fact, into Thea's lap.

Phi picked the weapon up without a moment's hesitation, got it pointed at his erstwhile captors, and advised them that if anybody moved, a goody-goody mama's boy would blow them straight to hell.

This was the scene that Thea saw when her blue eyes snapped open: Philo with the Yawkeys "covered," Genie sitting right beside him, panting but at ease.

To his own amazement, Phi was calm and thinking clearly; he felt that he could *handle* this. His number one concern was Thea's health and safety; number two was getting out of there. The first, he saw, was looking up; Thea'd come awake and now was smiling up at him. And as for number two . . .

"Let's lock them in their van," he said to Thea and the dog. They nodded their agreement mutely.

"Move," he told the Yawkeys, waggling the gun.

They moved, in silence, went outside, and climbed into the back part of the cargo van. Ed Yawkey, Senior, and his limping son appeared to be in shock. Only Deirdre found her tongue, just as the big side door slid shut.

"Your mama ought to be real proud of you," she told the boy.

In the Squareback, heading out of Acheron, Thea kept the sketch she'd done of Philo in her lap, smoothing it and smiling down at it. Philo stole some glances at it, too. So that's how I look to her, he thought. Not like a killer whale at all; she'd made his eyes all soft and light, enthusiastic, like a little boy's.

He'd said he'd call up Mrs. Cartwright once they reached the interstate and let her know that somehow, accidentally, the Yawkeys got locked inside their van. He figured she could get her nephew Scooter, who knew cars, to run out and release them.

Aside from that, he'd talked and talked about the things he'd thought about since leaving her, especially the stuff he'd come to realize while handcuffed to that iron ball all night. And he'd said he wanted her to come right home with him and meet his family; he was sure that they could all work something out.

Thea didn't jump right on that plan, which made him pretty nervous; she was in that quiet mode of hers again. But she *was* up front with him, while Genie stretched out in the back. And he recalled, if not any words, the *sense* of all she'd "said" when she first saw him in the Yawkeys' kitchen.

So, the way it seemed to him, she couldn't help but go along with his . . . well, *plan,* his happy ending for his trip. She loved him, she had said so, hadn't she? And she really had no other place to go.

On top of that, he also was her *hero,* now, he figured. As far as she knew, it was he who'd crippled big old Terry and disarmed Ed Yawkey, Senior. She'd been listening to tweetie-birds while acts 2 and 3 took place, and she had heard the last thing Deirdre Yawkey said to him.

If ever any girl had *ever* owed a guy . . .

Epilogue

It happened late that afternoon, as they were speeding north, still on the interstate. Phi heard the dog get up, but instead of lying right back down again, as usual, she sat straight up, right behind him; he could see her in the rearview mirror.

Then, she picked up a paw and laid it on his seat back, *tapped* his seat back, actually (he thought), as if it were his shoulder.

And, having gotten his attention, she began to make the oddest little sounds. At first he thought it was a yawn, but then he heard it as a canine version of that clearing-of-the-throat sound people make. Then she did it once again, and still another time.

He was looking in the mirror on those two occasions and both times, just as she made the noise, Genie also gestured with her chin, toward Thea.

Phi sighed, knowing what he had to do (or else?). But hey, he thought, he *was* a new man, after all. And, finally, in pursuit of happiness.

"Thea, honey," he began, "there's something that you ought to know, about what happened at the Yawkeys', how I came to have Ed's gun . . . ."

Genie lay back down again.